$\mathcal{S}$pirits
Between the Bays
Series

Volume VII

Up the Back Stairway

More True
Mid-Atlantic
Ghost Stories

Ed Okonowicz

Myst and Lace Publishers, Inc.

Spirits Between The Bays
Volume VII
Up the Back Stairway
First Edition

Published by
Myst and Lace Publishers, Inc.
1386 Fair Hill Lane
Elkton, Maryland 21921

Printed in the U.S.A.
by Victor Graphics

Artwork, Typography and Design
by Kathleen Okonowicz

Dedications

To
Mitch Radulski
My friend and cousin, who left us too soon.
Ed Okonowicz

To
My cousin, Linda Russell,
Thanks for your help.
Kathleen Burgoon Okonowicz

Acknowledgments

The author and illustrator appreciate the assistance of those
who have played an important role in this project.

Special thanks are extended to
the following friends for their assistance

including

John Brennan
Barbara Burgoon
Sue Moncure
Connie Okonowicz
Marianna Dyal
Ted Stegura
and
Monica Witkowski
for their proofreading and suggestions;

and, of course,

particular appreciation to the ghosts and their hosts.

Table of Contents

Legend and Lore

Site is open to the public.

Introduction

A nd so it begins, our journey to a new level of the bizarre, unusual and unexplained. Faithful readers of the *Spirits Between the Bays* series are familiar with our literary haunted house. They have seen the curtain pulled back (Vol. I), opened the door and were welcomed inn (Vols. II and III). They have passed through the vestibule and experienced the presence in the parlor (Vols. IV and V). And, in our last book, they stopped to hear the crying in the kitchen (Vol. VI).

Now, we journey to a higher level of horror and folklore as we explore the second floor of our haunted literary home.

In *Up the Back Stairway*, we deliver some of the region's most popular folktales and share more unusual true happenings, reported precisely as they've occurred to average, everyday people just like you.

In these pages we continue our 13-volume, horrific journey of the *Spirits* series. While reading these new tales, please notice that good ghost stories and unusual events are not restricted by geographic boundaries. Whether the bizarre experience happened in Raphine, Virginia—as occurred to my wife during our stay at the Oak Spring Farm last November—on the beaches of South Jersey, in the farmlands of Pennsylvania or in the wetlands of DelMarVa, the story should still be interesting to those who enjoy a good ghostly tale.

I have conducted hundreds of interviews and visited nearly a hundred haunted sites. That understood, I must add one final comment about the stories in this book. Each time we prepare a new volume, we try to offer the reader something a little different from what we've presented in the past. We approach each book with the hope that we will be able to come up with a new, bizarre story that we recognize as "a winner," that is a tale that goes well beyond "unexplained footsteps" and "slamming doors."

In this volume, I truly believe we have found such a haunted prize in the opening story, "No Room In the Inn." Not since the "Ghosts of Ashley Manor" have I been so uncomfortable during a site visit. I hope that you, too, will be very troubled by the events that happened, and are still occurring, in this home. I recommend that you read it late at night, when you are alone, when the weather is unsettled and the wind is blowing. I hope it raises goosebumps on your arms and makes your hair stand up—as mine did during the interview in this horrifying home. I hope this tale causes you to get up and call someone on the phone, hoping that the sound of another human voice will help ease your fear.

As always, we appreciate your patronage and value you as readers and the many of you that we have met as friends.

So, until we meet again in *Halloween House: A 2nd DelMarVa Murder Mystery* and Vol. VIII, *Horror in the Hallway* . . . .

Definitely, the Ghosts are Out There,

—Ed Okonowicz
in Fair Hill, Maryland,
at the northern edge
of the Delmarva Peninsula
--Spring 1999

No Room In The Inn

After I completed a book signing in Salem, New Jersey, at the Richard Woodnutt House Bed and Breakfast in the fall of 1998, I noticed a woman and young boy waiting for me near my car. Before I could say "Hello," they told me that their house was occupied by at least three ghosts and the mother added, "You just have to come over and see what you can do." Then, pointing at her 9-year-old son, she told me, "The Old Man threatened to drown my boy in the river. Now Billy won't even sleep in his bedroom."

Eventually, I arranged to visit the house, which is located somewhere in Salem County, New Jersey. More than that I will not share. It's an attractive and stately residence that could sit beside others of the same era and style in one of the older sections of any small, historic South Jersey town. But, it also might well be a solitary farmhouse, perched alone in the distance off a lightly traveled country road. The exact site doesn't matter—unless, one day it goes up for sale and you, unfortunately, happen to become its next owner.

To be fair to the current residents, who presently are involved in what might accurately be called a "physic residential dilemma," I want to be careful to offer no clue that might lead to the home's identification and eventual discovery.

During the last five years, I have conducted hundreds of interviews and visited scores of haunted sites. I honestly can say, not since the evening I spent in the 19th-century Federal mansion that resulted in the story, "The Ghosts of Ashley Manor" (in Pulling Back the Curtain, Vol. I), have I felt so uncomfortable during a site visit and interview.

So armed with my blessed rosary—that I placed around my neck and concealed beneath my shirt—and a vial of holy water—that I sprinkled in the passenger and rear seats of my car (I'm not kidding here, folks)—I drove across the Delaware Memorial Bridge and stopped in front of what I consider Salem County's ultimate haunted house. During the next two hours, at a kitchen table under a dim light, I listened to stories that were definitely horrifying, at times humorous and, I believe, completely true.

You decide for yourself.

I don't know if it was the freshly painted, wrap-around porch, the impressive turret or the ornately painted gables that first caught my attention. It doesn't matter. It definitely is an attractive house, one that had been built with care and pride by the craftsmen who had worked on its construction 140 years ago. They certainly would be happy that their efforts have been preserved and, as we approach the year 2000, the outstanding home still shows off its original dignity.

It was evening, about 7 o'clock in early December and the lights were on inside the home. A curtain was pulled back in one of the downstairs windows. They were waiting, obviously anxious to share their experiences. I, on the other hand, was equally eager to write them down.

"He's here!" someone shouted from inside the home. It was the voice of a young boy.

Within seconds the husband, who I had not yet met, greeted me on the brightly painted porch. "I'm Ralph," he said, extending his right hand and holding the door with his left hand as he ushered me inside. He was 45, tall, had lengthy brown hair and a dark mustache and beard. I later found out he worked as an accountant at a large manufacturing company.

We walked through the high-ceilinged entry hall. A set of stairs led to the upper level. We made a right turn, passed through the living room, and I could feel the warmth of the burning fireplace. Another quick turn delivered us into the kitchen. That's where I saw Pat, his wife and the woman I had met in Salem in early November, seated at the table.

She was in her early 40s, short, thin and had long black hair that reached to her shoulders. Pat said she worked part time as a school nurse for a few months each year.

Three children—Billy, their youngest; Taylor, 17, a high school junior; and Monica, a 20-year-old, who didn't want to talk to the "Exorcist Man," (that's how I was told she had described me)— were in their rooms and would be invited down to testify later.

It didn't take long for the stories to flow.

The facts and events were coming in such a rapid-fire speed that I asked Pat and Ralph to back up and start at the beginning. That was five years ago—in the summer of 1993. They lived in Philly and he worked in Cherry Hill. The congestion, traffic, noise and crime were getting old. After much discussion, they started looking for a place to live outside of the city. Like most people who decided to leave the rat race, they wanted to find an old home in a small town. Their second choice was a farmhouse in the country.

"When we passed by this house and saw the sale sign," Pat said, "we both agreed it was way out of our price range."

"There was no way we could afford it," agreed Ralph, jumping up, walking to the kitchen counter and bringing back a tray of silverware that he rested on the kitchen table.

"We rode around a bit, looked at some other properties, but couldn't find anything we really liked," Pat added. "After we were standing outside a house that was only about half the size as this one, Ralph mentioned this place to the real estate agent. I immediately said he was crazy, it probably was out of our league. But, the real estate agent called, told us the price—and it was cheaper than we could have hoped for—and she got us an appointment for the next day."

"We put in an offer," Ralph said, "and they accepted."

"How soon?" I asked.

"Immediately!" he answered, waving his hands in the air and raising his eyes toward the ceiling. "I mean, the yard and land itself was worth the price we got it for. We were thrilled."

Within two months the happy family was living in the new home, and things went fine until they decided to do some major remodeling, particularly moving around some bedrooms and changing the location of the living room and dining room.

"I heard that sometimes ghosts get upset when you change things around," Pat said, softly, leaning on the table and lifting her hand in a weary fashion. Of the two, she was the more sedate. Ralph was much more animated and excitable, and he became even more agitated as our evening together progressed and we got into the ghostly details of their home.

"After the changes," Pat continued, "things started to happen. The first thing I remember is that things began missing, or they would disappear and reappear. And we couldn't figure out why."

5

"Mostly shiny things," Ralph added, "CDs, car keys, things like that. They like shiny things," he said.

The children, who were from a previous marriage, would go away for the weekends. When they came back, the two boys and Monica would complain that someone had been into their things—jewelry, toys, collectibles—that had been left in their bedrooms.

"They started fighting with each other," Pat said, rolling her eyes. "I told them there was no way that things could have been taken, because no one was in the house except me and Ralph."

"We'd find CDs in the bathtub, on the floor in the back screened porch, all over the place. It was just nuts," Ralph added.

Then came the key incident, the first time, Pat said, that the ghosts were acknowledged and confronted.

The couple had returned home from shopping and Pat placed the car keys on the mantle in the living room, which by now had been newly located beside the kitchen. Less than a half hour later, Ralph said he had to go back out to pick up something they had forgotten to buy. But, when he reached for the keys, they were gone.

They both looked all over the living room—on the floor, in the fireplace itself, all over the kitchen. The car and house keys were nowhere to be found. It was as if they had simply disappeared—and within minutes of arriving home.

Shaking her head, Pat said, "I knew we had something in here before the key event happened. In fact, I had told Ralph, but he kept telling me I was crazy and looking at me like I was a nutcase."

Laughing from across the table, Ralph nodded and agreed. "That's right. I don't believe in this stuff. At least, I didn't then. I told her she was nuts."

"So," Pat continued, "I told him, 'Let me handle this.' Then, I screamed, 'Whoever took these damn keys, you've got 3 minutes to put them back. When I get back in here, they better be here! We're going for a walk in the back yard!'

"When we came back in," she said, smiling, "they were in the middle of the living room floor, and, yes, we had looked there."

"That's a fact," Ralph added, nodding his head.

"Then there were the spoons," Ralph said, shoving the tray of silverware he had pulled from the counter toward me.

I looked at the tray and about five of the spoons were bent in half.

Seeing the question written across my face, Ralph laughed, picked up one of the silver metal spoons—that had been bent at a right angle at the spot where the thin stem meets the bowl portion— and tossed it toward me.

"Right. Crazy isn't it?" he asked. "We will come down in the morning and there will be a half dozen of them, bent just like this, all over the counter. Now," he added, taking a spoon in his hands and bending it, "it takes a bit of effort to bend a spoon, wouldn't you say?"

I nodded agreement, then looked to my right at Pat.

"We just bend them back, now," she said, indicating that the spoon molestation was the least of their problems. But, they viewed the damaged flatware as proof that something strange happens in the home.

Laughing, Ralph added, "Now we just buy plastic spoons, and when they break them we throw them out."

"Why spoons?" I asked.

"Hey," Ralph said, smiling, "who knows? We thought you could tell us. You're the expert."

Explaining that the bent silverware was a first for me, we moved onto other events and sightings.

"Now, even after the keys and spoons," Ralph said, speaking as he carried the bent spoon tray back to the counter, "I'm still thinking my wife's nuts, see? But, I knew she wasn't crazy when I saw the Old Woman, that's what I call her. She floats around wearing a maroon dress with a gray apron, and sometimes it's the reverse. Then it's a gray dress with a maroon apron. It's old fashioned clothing, like from a hundred years ago. The first time I saw her, we had company in the living room. Another couple was here. As we are talking, I see this figure go up and down, up and down, three of four times, on the stairway. Now," he said, looking at me from across the kitchen table, "I don't say anything to anybody at the time, including my wife," he added, pointing toward Pat. "But, later, a few weeks later, she tells me she saw the same damn thing."

Pat agreed, explaining how she experienced the same sighting.

"But," Ralph added, laughing and waving his arms, "I'm still not a believer, not until I see the boy. The Kid is what I call him. I love the Kid. He's funny."

"He's only a little shit," Pat said. "His head only comes to the bottom of the fireplace mantel. He's dressed in a Little Lord

Fauntleroy outfit, with knickers, white socks and dark black shoes and a red velvet suit. Always wears the same thing."

Racing from the table, Ralph charged into the adjoining living room to act out the experience.

"He's a mover when he's excited," Pat said. "You better go and follow him." I did, but noticed that she stayed in her seat at the table.

As I entered the living room, Ralph was reclining on the couch, at the opposite end of the room from the hall entry doorway. He said he was there one night and thought he saw a shadow move from the entry hall doorway toward the kitchen entrance opening. But, when he turned whatever it was had disappeared.

"So I turned my head back, so I was facing straight ahead, still lying down," he said, "and I suddenly get this feeling like I'm being watched. And I look over to the side again, and this ghost, The Kid, is like standing six inches from my body, next to the sofa, and his head is leaning over looking down at me.

"I jump up and yell, 'Who the hell is this?' and, I swear," Ralph raised his hand as if taking an oath, "he runs away, toward the kitchen, with his head bent over. But the best one is, The Kid's laughing, and his head is bent and I can hear his shoes hit the wooden floor."

Suddenly, Ralph shot off the couch, ran across the room with his head bent and his back doubled over, imitating The Kid ghost. As he raced toward the entrance to the kitchen, following the same route as The Kid, Ralph laughed loudly, resembling an insane inmate or a Three Stooges scene, "HA HA HA HA HA HA HA HA!"

Back in the kitchen, with everyone again seated, Pat said, "He's a happy soul," referring to The Kid, not Ralph. "I've seen him in the basement," she added, "in the hall, in my daughter's room. One time I walked into Monica's room and he had her jewelry box on the floor and he was playing with the earrings and pins and lockets. All the shiny stuff he likes. You can see them, like they're real, and sometimes you can see through them. I shouted, 'Oh NO! If you want to play with it, then put it the hell back the way you found it!' I treat him just like a kid. That's what he is, a little kid.

"Then, he disappears and I pick it up and put it away. It will stay that way for about a month, then it will happen again. That's what the older kids yell about, their stuff being moved all around. But, I try to explain to them, it's the shiny stuff they like. Sometimes we find stuff all over. Sometimes we never find things. They just seem to disappear forever."

Laughing, Pat recalled the time she was washing dishes in the kitchen. It was about 4 o'clock in the afternoon and her towels and kitchen items kept being moved around. Suddenly, right behind her, The Kid shouted, "Ah HAH!"

It scared Pat so badly, that when she turned around and saw The Kid, she lost all control.

"I was chasing the goddamn ghost trying to catch him," she said. "I was determined to get him, and I ran after him all the way up the steps. I almost had him, but when I got to the top landing, he disappeared. I remember shouting to the boys, 'Where's he at? Where's he at?' "

The response of visitors to the unusual happenings in Pat and Ralph's home is quite different from that of the house's human residents.

One afternoon a friend of Pat's stopped by and the two women heard footsteps above, running down the upstairs hall. Eventually, the lady asked Pat who was making the noise. Pat said to just ignore the sounds. They happen occasionally.

After several more inquiries, Pat gave in and told her friend that "it's nothing to be concerned about, it's just one of the ghosts."

The lady immediately said, "I've got to go. I can't stay here, I just have to go."

And she hasn't been back.

While the children are in school and Ralph is at work, Pat spends a lot of time alone in the house.

"I wonder what's going to happen next," she admitted. "When I'm here alone, during the day, and they act up, I'll call him at work."

"I've got a 1-800 number," Ralph said, laughing, "so it gets a workout. You can imagine the bills I'd have if they were toll calls. But, I just tell her, take a walk, go shopping. What can I do?" he asked, tossing up his hands. "If I came home every time, I'd never be at work. Besides, by the time I got home, they'd be gone. And what could I do anyway?"

"The Kid doesn't bother me," Pat said. "The Old Lady doesn't bother me, but I'd like it if she'd pick up a dust rag and help me clean. Sometimes, she just sits in the kitchen and stares at me, but I try to ignore her. You can tell when she's around though, because she smells—like a rotten, sulfur smell, like the after smell of a burnt match. But the Old Man, he's the one I don't like, He's nasty. And the basement door is always locked, except that sometimes something breaks the lock off and opens the door. When that happens, there's serious trouble."

One month, Pat said she had to have the phone company come to her house four times to reattach wires that were continually being unfastened inside the phone box that was located in the basement.

Two times, Pat reattached the wires herself, But, soon afterwards, the ends were disconnected again and the metal cover was found on a shelf in the opposite end of the cellar—a place where it could not have fallen or rolled. The phone repairmen agreed, someone or something had to have disconnected the connections.

"When he goes into the basement," Pat said, pointing to Ralph, "he comes out a different person. It's as if the Old Man possesses him for a while. It could be a few hours or a few days. His face looks different, his eyes turn a different color. He even walks differently and smokes his cigarette differently. It's eerie."

Shrugging his shoulders and shaking his head, Ralph said, "I don't know what she's talking about. Seriously, I can't remember any of this, but I don't go down the basement anymore. Hardly ever."

One night, after Ralph had spent some time in the basement, he went upstairs and fell asleep while Pat was still downstairs. She said when she went to bed, after Ralph had already been asleep for several hours, Ralph woke up, stared at her and snarled, "It's about damn time you got into my bed!"

This was unusual, because each night Ralph would ask Pat the exact same thing, "Hi. Are you coming to sleep now?" It was just his way of saying good night.

In this instance, the snarling and the different words, which he repeated twice, made her realize that the Old Man had taken over her husband. She shook Ralph until he awoke and returned to his real nature. But, she admitted, it was one of her most unnerving experiences of all that had happened in their haunted house.

"I got one for you," Ralph said, "but first I have to explain, or describe the 'death chills.' That's what I call them, anyway."

At the other end of the table, Pat nodded and motioned for her husband to continue. "You'll love this," she added, shaking her head wearily.

By this time, I was running out of paper and my hand was getting tired from taking notes. There seemed to be no end to this fantastic fountain of the bizarre.

To summarize, the "death chills" occur when any of the three ghosts pass through one of the humans—namely Pat or Ralph. The kids didn't say that they had been subjected to this experience.

"It sucks the wind out of you," Ralph said. "The hair on the back of your neck and all over your arms stands up, 'cause you know it's coming. Then it feels like ice is going through you. It comes from the bottom of your feet and goes all the way up your body and exits your head or mouth. It's like the taste of a menthol cigarette. But the cold isn't coming from the outside, it's coming from the inside. It's like the cold is coming out of you not into you. Isn't that right?" he asked Pat.

"Yes," Pat said, nodding her head. "The first time I felt it, the Old Lady was on the stairs, blocking the way, and I tried to walk through her. I never did it again. It was a horrifying feeling. Now, you wait for them to go, or you ask them, 'Are you going up or coming down? I want to get by, now get out of the way.' "

"Do you walk by them if they move aside?" I wondered.

"No way," Pat said. "You can still catch a death chill. You have to wait for them to disappear, or yell at them to get out. But you don't go near them, unless you want to have a very uncomfortable experience."

Jumping up and running back into the living room, Ralph called me to follow, then told his favorite tale.

"It was 2 in the morning, one night," he said, standing in the middle of the room. "And I can't sleep. So I get up and come down here," he said, waving his arms, indicating the room. "And I hit the doorway, and stop under the door frame, and all three of them are down here—the Old Woman, The Kid and the Man—and I shout, 'EX-CUSE ME! I WANT MY ROOM BACK! IT'S MY ROOM!'

"They got up so fast and moved so fast, that they all went right through me. I got the death chill, three times after each other. It was their little joke, their way of getting back at me, I guess. I'll never forget that night. God, I hate that feeling."

They described The Man as old, with his gray hair pulled back, wearing black pants and a jacket, sort of like Amish clothing.

In the middle of one night, Pat heard her son Billy screaming in his room. When she entered, papers, toys, stuffed animals and books and clothing were flying around, as if a tornado had been let loose in the room.

11

As she ran in to get to her youngest son, she saw the outline of the Old Man to her left. Covering Billy with a blanket, Pat ran into the hall and slammed the door. The next day, she and Billy spent several hours restoring order in his bedroom—the one in which he refused to ever sleep in again.

"The dude was in there," Billy told me, as we talked at the kitchen table. "He told me he was going to drown me in the river. He had a deep voice, sort of like Darth Vader. I was scared, but I'm not afraid anymore. If I see him now, I just tell him to get lost."

Taylor, the high school junior, said he hadn't witnessed any of the ghosts, but he has lost a larger number of CDs and other items, including car keys, change and pens.

One night, Taylor's girlfriend was over, and they were watching television in the living room. She kept complaining that she was freezing and Taylor covered her with a blanket to help get her warm.

Laughing, Ralph said, "There was no way that the blanket was going to help. I walked through the room and, sitting on her other side, on the sofa, was The Kid, Little Lord Fauntleroy. No wonder she was freezing," Ralph said, laughing. "One of our ghosts was right beside her watching the TV. But, do you think I was going to say anything, like, 'Hey, the reason you're cold is because our Kid ghost is giving you a death chill?' No way. That would have gone over really great. So, I kept it to myself, until the next day when I told Pat. I figure we should feel lucky that the video didn't jump out of the player and fly across the room, like it does to us all the time. That would have scared the girl to death."

"Taylor doesn't see much because he keeps Jeb, our Doberman, in his room with him," Pat explained. "They definitely do not like that dog. Sometimes, when I can feel things starting to get ready to happen, I'll bring Jeb in to sit by me, and I won't have any problems. You can see his ears stand up, and his hair raised, and then he starts to snarl. Sometimes, he'll run through the house and stare at something that I can't see. It's good he's around."

Pacing across the kitchen, Ralph asked me, "Does this sound crazy to you? I mean, have you ever heard anything like this before in your whole life? You talk to people, tell me the truth. Are we nuts? Are there other people like us out there? Are you going to leave here and think we're crazy? Because all this happened. I mean, this isn't Amityville, but we've gotta be right up there with it. What do you think?"

I told them that of all the haunted sites I'd visited, their home was up there with such noteworthy troubled sites as Ashley Manor, Fort Delaware, the Cecil County Detention Center that's built over an Indian burial ground and the troubled parsonage on Maryland's Eastern Shore.

I got the impression that they were both happy that they weren't crazy but also troubled that they had purchased a home that would be difficult to unload, if they ever decided to do so.

"We put everything we had into this house," Pat said. "There's no way we'll be able to move. I just want to understand what is going on. I called the former owner, but she said, 'No. I never saw anything,' but I find that very hard to believe."

Ralph said the grandson of the previous owner had come over to play with Billy.

"We call him the 'Demon Seed,' " Pat said, laughing. "He's a little troublemaker. He's so bad that Jack the Ripper would be nicer than that kid. He was eating dinner here one night and I asked him if he ever missed anything. And he said, 'Oh, yeah, and sometimes we would have the windows open when we got home, and we know that we shut them before we left. But, my mom told me never to talk about any of that.'

"We asked the nearby neighbors," Pat continued, "but all they could say is that whoever lived in this house fought horribly. And, I tell you, sometimes, when the ghosts are around, we fight like hell. That's all we have been able to find out."

"Except," Ralph added, "the area historian said he heard an old lady fell in the basement and broke her neck. So that might be the Old Woman."

"Yeah," Pat interjected, "we asked the historian, Horace, if anybody ever died in this house. And he said, 'Hell! The house is 140 years old. Of course somebody died there.' But I think The Kid is one of the builder's children. There's a graveyard near here with all the original owner's family buried there, and I swear that The Kid ghost belongs in there with them.

"I want to find out who they are, where they are buried and why they died. That's all."

"But The Kid, you can tell that he doesn't want to leave," Ralph said. "He likes it here, and I like the kid. He can stay."

"And the Old Woman can stay, too," Pat said. "But it really gets to me when she comes and sits in the kitchen, in that chair and just stares at me. It seems that she does it whenever I get behind in my house cleaning. I get so mad that I look at her and say, 'You know you're dead! You know you stink? You know you give me the creeps! What do you want?' After a while, she just sort of fades away.

"My mother tells me I should ask what her problem is. I should say, 'Can I help you?' And say, real nice, 'You know, you're really dead.' Like I want to go around my house all day talking to someone who's dead.

"My sister, before she comes over, calls now and asks, 'Are they up and about?' Like I can predict their schedule."

Like others who find themselves in this bizarre situation, Pat and Ralph are torn between living with the known or taking a chance on having the house cleansed. Unfortunately, there is no guarantee that such a ceremony would work. In fact, it could make matters worse.

"People have told me to get a priest in here. I already have holy water and a crucifix in every room, but that hasn't stopped anything," Pat said.

She looked weary as we wrapped up the evening. I realized that she and her husband had shared only a sampling of their experiences during the two-hour interview. There was much more to tell, but nothing that would make a difference in their situation. They still were trapped in a haunted house.

"I think it's best to leave well enough alone," she said. "I could live like this. I don't want it to get any worse."

Ralph agreed, "I'm an Italian Catholic. I'm afraid of it and what it can do. I don't want to open up the Gates of Hell. I don't want to make the thing mad. If I bring in a voodoo witch, who knows what could happen? I'm afraid to have a seance and open up that door to the other side. We might get more than we can handle."

Laughing, he opened his arms wide, "We're full now! Five living and three dead are enough!"

"I can't have anymore," Pat said, shaking her head and rolling her tired eyes. "There's no more room in the inn."

Fantom Friend and Foes

In the back of each of our ghost books is a form that encourages those who have stories they would like to share to provide a name and phone number. Toward the end of 1997, Sabrina's note arrived in the mail. She indicated she had a number of experiences and I gave her a call. Following a lengthy telephone conversation, she sent me a letter that confirmed some of the information she had shared and adding a few additional interesting incidents.

At first, Sabrina's stories seemed to focus on nothing more than a few bumps in the night and mysterious smells in her kitchen. But, as the saga developed, her experiences were anything but ordinary.

In her early 30s, Sabrina lives in the southern part of New Castle County, Delaware. She is married and strikes you as an average, pleasant working wife. No third eye. No black pointed hat and broom. No black cat resting beside her feet. Like many people, she believes in ghosts. Unlike most people, Sabrina is not afraid to speak her mind openly and honestly.

It all started in Hockessin, Delaware, when she was a bit younger.

"I want you to understand, I've been involved with ghosts for some time," she said, her voice calm, smooth and steady. "In fact, the 'first' ghost I ever encountered was that of my grandmother, on my father's side. I was pretty close to her as a girl. She used to make clothes for me and baby-sit me. She also used to visit and sleep over on Christmas Eve. When she died, I took it pretty hard."

Hesitant to let go of her attachment, Sabrina explained that she kept a box filled with her grandmother's jewelry and other personal items.

"After she died, some of us in the family noticed strange goings-on in our house. Things would disappear and then show up in odd places. There were smells of food cooking—usually popcorn or waffles and sometimes peanut butter—but there was nothing open and nothing on the stove. Then, there was the sound of footsteps in the attic."

Since the entrance to the attic was through Sabrina's closet, she heard the footsteps directly above her bed at night, when she was trying to sleep.

"My younger sister came up with the idea that it was a ghost, who she named 'Ghost of John.' Somehow, this seemed to make the idea of a ghost easier to deal with," Sabrina said, smiling slightly. "I didn't think about who the ghost was at that time. It was only later that I figured that the ghost was probably my grandmother."

By the time Sabrina moved out a few years later, the entire family knew when the ghost was around. The key indicator was the smell of cooking.

"One night," she recalled, "when I was living in my apartment in Newark, I smelled the cooking, and I knew the ghost was there, in my apartment, with me. By that time, I wasn't afraid, because I was convinced that it was my grandmother.

"I was so startled that the ghost was there, and that it had left my parent's house and followed me, that I woke up my husband. He smelled the cooking, too."

Sabrina said there was no way the odors could have come from a neighboring apartment, especially since all of the rest of the tenants, both upstairs and down, worked during the day. They would not have been up at 3 in the morning making a snack.

"My husband is a skeptic when it comes to weird things happening," Sabrina said, shaking her head. "He smelled it, too, and had to contend with the fact that it was really happening. He could offer no logical explanation. I was convinced that my grandmother had come to live with me. And, as it turned out, she had come to stay."

Sabrina said both she and her husband, Len, would smell cooking from time to time. He told Sabrina her grandmother was there to watch over her, like a guardian angel. This made sense, since Sabrina had been going through a rough period, and she said she had been under a tremendous amount of pressure at that time.

"One night, I went into the kitchen," Sabrina said, "and there she was. My grandmother was standing at the stove, but when I tried to talk to her she ignored me."

Interestingly, Sabrina said the kitchen she saw was not in her apartment—it was from her grandmother's kitchen. The entire scene was hazy, as if it were a picture from the past.

"I had forgotten what it looked like," Sabrina said, referring to her grandmother's kitchen. "But I recognized it right away, even though I was in a shock.

"I should add that when her husband died, my grandmother had to bake goods and sell them to survive. I guess that's how she got into cooking so much. I talked to her that night. I thanked her for being around when I needed her, and I told her I loved her very much. But, I said I felt responsible that she was sticking around taking care of me when she could be moving on.

"I told her I would be okay if she went to rest, that I had Len to take care of me now. But," Sabrina paused, "I also told her that I would miss her terribly. And, when I finished, she turned and looked at me for a long moment, and then the whole scene faded and . . . she was gone. I know she still does pop in once in a while, but it's only for a night."

The second encounter was not as pleasant.

Len and Sabrina moved to Bridgeville, Delaware, an agricultural area in the southern end of the state. They rented a large old house on South Main Street that was built in the late 1800s, just before the turn of the century, and it had an interesting appearance. They also realized that it was much larger than the two of them needed.

"I didn't like the house the moment I saw it," Sabrina said, "but Len's heart was set on it, so I went along with the whole deal."

The house had not been occupied for several years.

"As soon as we were moved in," Sabrina said, "I immediately felt the sense of dread that surrounded the house. But, at that time, I wasn't able to figure out why I had this uneasy feeling. I thought it was just because I was in a new area, with people I didn't know, and that the bothersome feeling would go away. Unfortunately, it didn't."

After a few months, Len's mother gave the couple two small kittens. They were very affectionate, Sabrina recalled, and they would curl up in her lap and follow her everywhere.

"At first, I didn't make the connection," she said, thinking back to the fall of 1992, when she lived in the old home. "Soon, we noticed that they refused to be out in the rest of the house when we went to bed. If one of them didn't make it into our bedroom before the lights were out and we shut the door, they would cry until one of us got to them. Also, they refused to go into the basement, although they were fine exploring the rest of the house—in the daylight, of course."

But, the hesitancy to go into the sublevel of the house was something that Sabrina and the cats had in common.

"I was deadly afraid of the basement," she admitted. "It had an open crawl space. The first time I walked past that thing, I was so upset and afraid, I almost just turned and bolted. It gives me the chills just remembering."

Unless her husband was with her, Sabrina would not go into the basement. She said he also admitted that the area bothered him, too, especially the crawl space.

"It didn't take long to determine that there were 'ghosties' in the building," Sabrina said. While the pace of her conversation had increased, her voice had gotten a little softer.

She and Len began to mark down the strange events they noticed—uneasy feelings, temperature changes and strange behavior of the cats.

"We finally decided there were probably two ghosts," she said. "One seemed to stay in the basement and the other stayed with us. We asked around Bridgeville, but people were reluctant to tell us anything, other than the house had had quite a few occupants, and it had been empty for about two years—until we came along."

Finally, the wife of Len's boss, who was active in the historical society, told the young couple that a former owner had been an alcoholic and his wife had committed suicide by hanging herself in the basement.

"That made sense to us," Sabrina said. "The upstairs ghost was the husband and the basement ghost was the wife. She had experienced a tragic death and was trying to scare us. I remember there were times when the husband ghost would actually brush up against us. We could feel it. It was like there was a rush of energy from somewhere out of the blue."

After they found out the source of their problems, the situation in the haunted house seemed to get worse.

"You would think that, knowing the ghosts were there," Sabrina said, "you could prepare yourself, or fortify yourself against them. If anything, the whole atmosphere got twisted. Len and I began having the most vicious and disturbing fights, which became increasingly violent on both of our parts."

Sabrina said they had been involved in fights and arguments before, but the ones in the Bridgeville house were nothing like they had experienced.

"One night," she said, "my husband destroyed a room. I mean, he broke the furniture and hurled stuff everywhere. This was NOT how I had ever seen him act. It was totally out of character. I wasn't even sure I knew who he was then, and he said the same of me for that period of time."

Sabrina said there were pictures taken while they lived in the house, but the two of them look different—weird, evil.

"It kind of scares me now to look at these pictures of myself," she said. "I am inclined to think that this house has some kind of continuing loop that mirrors the ghost's lives, and that anyone living there gets sucked up into it. Our landlady and her husband had been the last occupants, and after living there a year or two they divorced. During our stay, they became reunited. But, they don't live there anymore."

One of the most horrifying events occurred one night when Len wasn't home. Sabrina recalled that one of the cats was crying, and she went into the living room to give the animal some attention.

"She was standing in the middle of the room, looking at the corner ceiling," Sabrina said. "She had a horrified look on her face. I know that sounds silly, but there's no other way to describe it. She was scared stiff. I looked in the direction that she was looking, and that's when I saw it—or her.

"It was the wife ghost. She was sitting in mid-air near the ceiling. She had on a housedress with flowers, and her hair was floating above her, like she was in the water or something. Her face was twisted in a grotesque, frightening expression. She looked like something out of a nightmare. I stood there for a moment, frozen in fear and shock. Then, I grabbed the cat and shouted at the ghost to stop scaring my kittens. I bolted for the bedroom where I stayed for the rest of the night.

"It was the only room where I felt safe. The kitten never got more than an inch from my side the rest of the night. I really couldn't blame her."

After a year and a half, Len, Sabrina and the cats moved out.

"We couldn't take it. We broke the lease and left. By the way, the house had been for sale the entire time we were there, and I saw people come in who refused to enter the basement. That door was just inside the back entrance. I saw people come inside the back door and turn right around and leave and refuse to enter that house. I mean, the house needed work, but that was unusual behavior."

Sabrina said things got better for everyone immediately after they left the haunted house.

Smiling, she added, "The cats stopped sleeping with us right after we moved out, and they don't cry in the middle of the night anymore, either."

Tombstone Tale

I discovered a message on my e-mail screen early in the fall of 1998. The writer resides in Cecil County, Maryland, and her old farmhouse is located off a narrow country lane somewhere in the triangle formed by Rising Sun, Perryville and Elkton.

The building's original foundation remains, but modern siding and improvements over the years have altered the structure's original appearance significantly. Located in the rear of the property is a large barn, its panels weathered gray and white from the passing seasons. A few old outbuildings also dot the acreage.

For the purposes of our story, we'll say the writer's name is Lisa. Rarely would—or should—one who lives in a haunted residence want his or her real name and address used. (Inns, restaurants and museums, on the other hand, proudly advertise their haunts—and who would blame them? The more ghosts, the better for business.)

But, as you read the letter that begins on the following page, you will see that Lisa and her troubled family are not looking for attention . . . rather they are seeking answers.

Sept. 3, 1998

Ed,

I briefly met you at the Ghost Tour at Fort Delaware, and told you that I would write to you about things that have happened at my home.

Here goes . . . first the facts.

I moved into this home seven years ago. This is a very old house, an architect told me it was at least 150 years old.

Simple background . . . .

I am not "into ghosts," by no means. I've never searched them out, and my engineering mind tries very hard to give me logical "answers" to my strange happenings. It is only after seven full years that I can conclude some things are very ghost-like at this home.

When we first moved here, we found a child's tombstone in the barn. I was six months pregnant at the time, and my husband said, "Wow, the spirit wants to take over the body of a new baby."

I didn't find this funny at all and would have quickly moved into an apartment and lose our $500 deposit. The former quickly residents assured me that a previous homeowner used to make cemetery headstones and this must have been a "typo." I bought the story and we moved in.

Years later I read about a lady, who for years had used grave-stones in her yard for Halloween decorations. The neighbors complained and, after investigating, the police found out they had been stolen from a cemetery. She had purchased them from a flea market and was told they were simply "misprints." So now, looking back, I don't know about our tombstone, but we threw it away.

Okay, now the ghost stuff . . . .

The upstairs bedroom, my bedroom, has always been creepy, but I have never SEEN anything. My husband worked nights, I had two new babies, so I simply slept downstairs for a couple years when he was away.

The first weird event involved a nice, roly-poly, older gentle-man, who was our exterminator. His name was John. He would come regularly and spray, and he always did the outside and perimeter before entering the house. If we were not home, we would leave the door unlocked for him.

On this particular day, he arrived and sprayed the outside, then went into the basement. When he was down there, he heard a lot of walking going on upstairs. He said later that he could tell exactly where this "person" was walking.

He assumed that, although there were no cars in the driveway, that either my husband, Mike, or myself had come home. When he came inside the house to spray, he yelled for one of us. When no one answered, he said he thought that he had scared a burglar. So, "armed" with his bug sprayer, he searched the whole house, and found no one. Back at the office, he told his fellow workers. They convinced him that he was obligated to call and tell me what had happened.

After John called, I knew that it was not just me, being scared to be alone. Something else was going on.

I started attending a church that was big on women being "godly and submissive." I figured that I was not being submissive and proper, if I was sleeping with the children. So I began to FORCE myself to sleep upstairs.

At this same time, we were installing a stove pipe through the bedroom floor, and I had heard that spirits became unsettled during renovations. A number of different things happened upstairs at that time. I will probably bore you, but here's what I recall.

•There were several "flashes." They seemed like camera flashes, as if you were lying down with your eyes shut, trying to fall asleep, and someone took a "flash" picture of you. Or, it was as if someone turned the overhead light on and off real quickly. I would open my eyes, and it was as if you could still see the flash after it happened. I would see an initial flash and then see the remnants of it. There were several of these instances.

•There also were sounds of balls being bounced down the bedroom steps. But the ball did not sound like a "now a day" ball that you would buy at a grocery store. It sounded like the "old time" thick rubber, approximately 9-inch ball. It sounded more like a thumpy ball and not like a pingy ball.

•One night I was downstairs reading, and all the kids were asleep. I remember it was a Monday or Tuesday, and I was just getting around to reading the Sunday paper. There was this awful crash upstairs, in the attic. I was *so* sure that it was a person that I called the police at 911. I searched the whole attic with a gun, then the police arrived and did a "half search." Neither of us found anything, and nothing had even fallen out of place.

•One afternoon, I was painting the upstairs bedroom. There was nothing in the room except me, paint and a stepstool. I was up on the ladder and heard papers fall. I got down and nothing had fallen, there were no papers in the room. As soon as I began to paint again, I heard the same noise repeated.

•In several instances, the light would be on when I had not left it on. Or, I would leave the house and drive away and the upstairs light would be on. I would go to bed and the attic light would be on. These things happened repeatedly.

By this time I had told several people and everyone thought it was funny. This one guy at work, Terry, thought it was neat. He came over one night. We were standing in my kitchen and, as he got ready to leave, he asked, "Hey, do you still hear your noises from upstairs?"

On cue, the "ball sound" came down the steps. He walked over, and surprised he said, "Hey, there is nothing here. No ball!"

I was like, "Terry, that is what I've been telling you. This is what always happens."

He spoke loudly and said, "Okay, that was pretty good, but if you could do something right NOW, then we would believe in you . . . ."

Right then, on cue again, my son's toy ice cream truck played the entire ice cream melody. Terry and I ran to the living room to find the toy at the bottom of the toy box and could not get it to make the sound again, ever. We even unscrewed the back and wiggled the battery. A week or so later, I threw they toy away.

I spoke to the women from my church and the minister. I wanted to do the biblical thing.

They suggested that I walk around my house and state my faith, and if I heard anything to "announce my alliance to Christ." I did so, and have not heard anything since.

Every now and then the light will be on or I will see a "flash," while I am in my bed. But, all and all, nothing really happens anymore.

Hope this can help you, it was really creepy writing all this. My hands are sweaty as I type. I hope that I don't get "them" all stirred up again. Write and tell me what you think.

Lisa

After the Letter

Since receiving this letter, I met Lisa and her children. They are your average, everyday, run-of-the-mill family, except they probably live with a ghost.

The house is old and she said the base of the tombstone is still in the barn, except now it's used as a step to access a raised level of the building. But, she said her husband got rid of the top, inscribed section long ago.

Since writing the letter, however, things have not remained totally calm.

Lisa had mentioned about hearing sounds, but rarely seeing evidence or results of the noises. On one recent occasion, she was reading and heard a loud crash from another room. Accustomed to such "nonevents," she did not bother to investigate immediately. But, when she later passed the room from which the noise had occurred, a large bookcase had fallen, or been knocked, over.

"I was happy to see it tipped over," Lisa said. "The noises happen so much anymore that we don't even investigate, because there's never anything disturbed."

Lisa said her husband is relaxed about the unusual events and doesn't get upset.

"He believes there's something here," she said, "but it doesn't seem to bother him. I don't want to believe it's something not biblical. I'm a Christian. I know Satan can take other appearances. If so, why is he here? The last time it was hot and heavy was when I was joining the church. My husband is getting more into the church now, and maybe that's why things are getting stirred up, because of that. I just don't know."

Possible Explanation

The presence of the initial tombstone cannot be ignored. The old grave marker makes one think that, perhaps, the property had been the site of an old family graveyard that had been plowed over many years ago.

Lisa is checking old historic records at the local historical society to see what she can find.

But, is the presence of an unmarked and long-forgotten gravesite a real possibility, or is it just one of those overused, trite and common explanations that most people toss out but is rarely the case?

After all, how many unmarked graveyards can there really be?

Keep in mind that in *Opening the Door*, Vol. II of our *Spirits* series, it is mentioned that the Dill family in Kent County, Delaware, did a thorough investigation of historical records of that First State county and found 379 burial sites listed—in that one small county. However, they physically were only able to locate 229—leaving 150 unmarked cemeteries still unaccounted for and undiscovered.

Without serious research or effort, in three recent newspaper articles—all published within a short, six-day period from Nov. 27 to Dec. 1, 1998—these related stories were found.

Headline

"Hundreds of graves uncovered: Construction site may yield 600 more"

Wilmington News Journal, Nov. 27, 1998

Summary

In Wilmington, Delaware, more than 2,260 graves were uncovered at a hospital construction site, and officials think that another 600 remain. The interesting thing about the article is that it is a continuation of a story that broke in the summer when the large unmarked and apparently forgotten cemetery site was discovered in downtown Wilmington during construction of a hospital addition. However, of particular interest is the fact that the graveyard had been in use from the 1840s through the 1930s.

This was not an out-of-the-way, hamlet plot used in the 1800s by a long-forgotten, low-profile farm family.

Headline

"Couple's home on graveyard"
Associated Press story in the Cecil Whig, Nov. 30, 1998

Summary

A family in Bishopville, Maryland, discovered a hip joint, a femur and a casket handle in their front yard and started to believe rumors that their home "really was sitting on top of an old graveyard." The short article added that the discovery of the remains has helped the present owners understand the strange noises the family hears in their home at night.

The family wants the graves removed, but Worcester County officials apparently want to repave the road in front of the home, "further burying the graves."

The family has filed a lawsuit against the developer's estate.

Headline

"Nanticoke burial site falls into disrepair: Leaders want state to turn over control"
Wilmington News Journal, Dec. 1, 1998

Summary

The assistant chief of the Nanticoke Indians has found scattered remains of his ancestors at the state-owned Thompson Island Preserve outside Dewey Beach, Delaware. The Nanticoke burial site has fallen into disrepair and tribal members are demanding, according to the article, "stewardship of a 20-acre parcel to protect the graves from future erosion or desecration."

These few examples reinforce the fact that unmarked gravesites are more numerous and commonplace than imagined, that some known sites are subject to misuse, vandalism and poor care and, in some cases, owners of homes built on or near graveyards claim to have witnessed unusual, unexplained and bizarre experiences.

Happy house hunting.

Red Rose Inn

For several years, people have asked me, "Are you going to write about the Red Rose Inn?" Located about eight miles beyond the Mason-Dixon Line, and just above the northern border of Delmarva, the inn was on my list. I arranged to visit the historic site on the day after Thanksgiving. Early on that Friday morning, as waitstaff and cleaning personnel were restoring order after serving 500 dinners the previous holiday, I met with owner Lee Covatta in the building's Carriage Lounge.

Lee explained that she and her husband, Richard, had purchased the business 14 years ago. They operate the site with their son, Anthony. And, yes, they were aware of the stories of the establishment's resident ghosts. But that didn't bother them. Lee smiled, adding that her brother's restaurant business, also located in Pennsylvania, has experienced more spirit activity than has ever been reported at the Red Rose Inn.

History and the Name

During Colonial times, present day U.S. Route 1 was the only main road connecting Philadelphia and Baltimore. In its earliest days, it was little more than a narrow path that was dusty in summer and wet and rutted during winter rain and snow.

Travelers, both on foot and horseback, followed the well-used trail, as did wagons and stagecoaches. At periodic distances, inns and waystations to care for animals and horses, sprang up, but they were few and far between.

Crossing this northeast-southwest route was the north-south Indian trail that is present day Route 796. This two-lane road, that passes beside today's 1740 Room in the inn, was originally used by hunting parties of the Delaware and Lenni Lenape tribes. The route was important as braves traveled back and forth to the hunting grounds along the watersheds that flowed into both the Susquehanna and Delaware Rivers.

In 1740, nearly 260 years ago, the oldest portion of the Red Rose Inn was built near the popular crossroads to serve area settlers, travelers and Indians.

In the Red Rose Inn brochure, it states, "It became a meeting place where the drover and the farmer could transact business; where the Indian could trade coonskin for gunpowder; and where food and drink could provide hearty fare before a warming fire."

During its history, the inn has hosted some noteworthy guests, including Helen Keller, the Grand Duchess Charlotte of Luxembourg, various U.S. Senators and Congressmen, and numerous royal visitors from Europe.

Additions have increased the size of the building, and the Carriage Lounge was formerly the Carriage House. Interestingly, while the building has grown, the 17th-century land grant has been reduced from its original 5,000 acres to the present 5 acres that surround the building.

The Red Rose Inn's distinctive name is much more significant than one might initially imagine. The property was deeded to William Penn, founder of Pennsylvania, through a land grant from King Charles II in 1681.

According to the "History of the Tavern House in Jennersville Now Known as the Red Rose Inn," written in 1980 by David E. Conner and provided by the owner, Penn divided the land into counties. The County of Chester, named for Cheshire, England, was the southeastern-most county in the present day boundaries of Pennsylvania. Because of a dispute with the Calverts of Maryland, the Mason-Dixon survey of 1763 verified that the land belonged to Penn and established the formal, present-day boundary between the two colonies.

In 1731, William Penn's sons—John, Thomas and Richard Penn—deeded 5,000 acres to William Penn of London, grandson of the founder of Pennsylvania.

"The deed stipulated," Conner wrote, " 'his heirs and assigns forever pay one Red Rose, on the 24th day of June, if same be demanded.' This type of deed was the continuation of an almost extinct medieval custom. In the middle ages, a feudal Lord would often grant a piece of land to a vassal or knight in return for military service. As it became less necessary for these feudal lords to defend their land with military strength, it became common practice to extract a token payment of rent for a grant of land. Often the payment was a spade of earth, or an indigenous fruit, nut or flower. Although these deeds are fairly common in England, only two are known to exist in America. The deed to the 5,000-acre tract deeded to William Penn, the grandson, contains the quit-rent provision."

The painting of three red roses, hanging above the fireplace in the parlor dining room, symbolizes the original land payment agreement. Some residents of the Jennersville-Kelton area recall a time when there was an annual rose-payment ceremony held at the inn each year on the 24th of June.

The Haunts

"They say a little girl was murdered by an Indian, and they thought it was sometime in the 1700s," Lee said, recalling what she has heard about the inn's resident ghosts. "Some say he was hanged, wrongly, and buried in the cellar."

Is it true that their spirits still haunt the building?

"Some say so," Lee replied. "They say that's why the little girl remains with the building. That's the basic story about why it's haunted. There are people who claim to have seen the little girl walking around, near the ladies room on the main floor. That was about 10 years ago. They said they saw a cute, little blond girl in a white dress float toward the ladies room. But when they went to look, there was no one there. I haven't seen her. There have been other types of sightings."

I asked her to share what she had heard.

Some of the sightings, she explained, were seen by the inn's bartenders and patrons late in the evening, around 10 o'clock near closing time. All of the entrances are locked at that time, except the one going out from the Carriage Lounge.

"Several times older ladies, and one time an older gentleman, have just appeared here in the lounge," Lee said, pointing to an area between the edge of the bar and restrooms. "People have been sitting here at the bar. Now," smiling, she added, "perhaps they've had a few drinks that have added to their imagination, but the bartenders will look up and ask, 'Can I help you?' or 'Where did you come from?' Then, the visitor just vanishes.

"They say it's really creepy seeing someone there and watching them vanish into thin air. Then they ask the patrons if they saw anything, and they answer, 'Yeah! Where did they come from?' or 'Where did they go?' "

Lee said that while she has not seen anything mystical, she has witnessed the results of ghostly activity.

One night, she had completed setting up for a wedding that was to take place the next day in the Parlor. Under the painting of the three red roses, she carefully decorated the mantel. Since the ceremony was to take place in the room, she wanted everything to be perfect and an appropriate and proper setting for the special event.

"I locked up, and when I came in Saturday morning, the picture was on the floor and it took everything down with it. But," Lee stressed, "the picture was not damaged. It wasn't as if it fell off the wall. The nail was still in the wall, the wire was still attached on the back of the painting. It was as if it was placed on the floor in front of the fireplace undamaged. But, everything else that I had tried to do was ruined and knocked over."

On one occasion, a writer from the Kennett Square newspaper had interviewed Lee for an article about the inn and its ghosts.

"She was a regular customer," Lee recalled, "so I knew her well. She brought in a parapsychologist from a college in Pennsylvania who said she believed there were sprits here. The writer went home and, since she wasn't on a tight time schedule, didn't complete the article immediately. Each night afterwards, she heard banging against the side of her house. But there were no shutters and no shrubs, nothing that should cause it. When she completed the article, the banging stopped.

"In the gift shop, we had a table in the center with a long tablecloth that fell all the way to the floor. There were lots of dolls in the shop. One day, we went in and could not find any dolls. They all had disappeared. After a thorough search, we found them all under the table. There were dozens of dolls hidden behind the long tablecloth.

"It was as if a little girl had been playing with the dolls."

According to Lee, there was more activity 10 years ago.

"When we first came in, there seemed to be a lot of movement. Now, I think everybody's happy. When we came in we were redecorating, moving pictures and items around. We would put something up and the ghost would take it down. I guess it eventually decided to live with what we're doing and has finally settled down."

Lee stressed that there have never been any problems or negative feelings associated with the inn's unseen guests.

"People who come here to eat or spend the night say there's a comfortable feeling here. Our overnight guests say, 'It's like being home at mom's.' I think our building is very protected by those spirits who reside here."

Lee said it's not unusual for customers to ask if there are ghosts present in the inn.

"People will come in and say, 'Show us where the ghosts are!' Over the years, I've noticed that when you're discussing ghosts there are two types of people—those who run out the front door and those who want to hear more. The way I figure it, those who are scared away probably shouldn't haven't been here in the first place."

Reflecting on the building's colorful history and present use, Lee said it's interesting and satisfying that in its earliest days the inn was a central site where people gathered for trading, meeting, eating and lodging.

"Today," she said, "we're still doing the same thing. We're halfway between Philadelphia and Baltimore. We're in the middle of nowhere, and yet we're centrally located, and it's still a gathering place for that very reason. Yesterday, we had people come from all over, and many were from families scattered in different areas who met here to celebrate Thanksgiving together."

Features: The historic building is filled with antiques that Lee has purchased on her travels. Price tags are attached to wall hangings and furniture, indicating that items are for sale. This includes just about everything except things that were in the building at the time of the Covatta family's purchase. A gift shop, featuring hand-crafted pieces from area artisans, is located on the first-floor, in the 1740 Room. This is the oldest section of the building that was the original trading post. A large mural—approximately 6 feet x 20 feet—in the large dining room depicts the payment of one red rose as annual rent. The Brandywine Lounge, a downstairs night-club, features live entertainment three nights a week. Fireplaces are located in nearly every dining room. Note the small ceramic emblem cemented into the stonework above the walk-in fireplace in the Fireside Room. Years ago, this was a common practice by artisans who were proud of their work and wanted it identified.

The inn also offers overnight accommodations in a number of comfortable guest rooms on the upper level. The Star Rose Memorial Gardens are a half block from the inn.

Sightings/Activity: In the Carriage Lounge; in the Parlor Room; near the Ladies Room in the vicinity of the large, first-floor dining room; in an upstairs window facing south. In the Billiard Room area of the lower level, cuts in the rock foundation indicate a possible hiding place for slaves who used the site as a stop on the Underground Railroad. There also is a legend that the body of an Indian was buried in the basement.

Contact: 804 West Baltimore Pike, West Grove, PA 19390 (mailing address), located in Jennersville at the intersection of U.S. Route 1 and Route 796; telephone, (610) 869-3003.

Philip's Personal Parlor

Many of the large houses on Newton Street in Salisbury, Maryland, were built during the Victorian era or in the early years of the 20th century. Their ornate architectural characteristics command attention, and many passersby reflect fondly on the craftsmen who created these magnificent, 100-year-old structures.

It's little wonder that some former residents, even after they have gasped their last earthly breath, have been reluctant to leave certain homes in this historic Delmarva city. This is one of those stories.

In the early 1980s, Laura moved into a three-story, five-bedroom mini-castle, complete with three fireplaces, a wrap-around porch and stained-glass windows. Soon after the single, freelance writer and English teacher—with no pets or children—had set up house, she started experiencing unusual "activity." Unexplained footsteps on the backstairs, near the formal parlor, made her begin to think that she wasn't alone.

"It didn't bother me," she said. "My father and grandfather had told me ghost stories since I was old enough to listen. Also, I had written about cults in big cities and I had experienced a number of unusual events during my life. I really found what was happening rather interesting, so I decided to wait to see what was going to occur next."

Shortly after renting her empty rooms to a few female college students, Laura heard noises on the backstairs. Thinking her young tenants were causing the disturbance, she went to investigate and found there was no one else in the house.

"This happened several times during the next few months, while I was the only person in the house," Laura recalled. "Then, I noticed that my unseen friend was starting to make his decorating preferences known. If he didn't like the artwork I had hung above the mantle in that back parlor, it would come crashing down in the middle of the night."

It wasn't just paintings that seemed to bother Laura's resident ghost; knickknacks placed on the fireplace mantle would be found shattered on the floor on the other side of the room.

"Kerosene lamps, small figurines," Laura said, "if he didn't like them, they would be hurled across the parlor. I could tell they just didn't fall off the mantle, because you would find marks on the opposite wall where the object had been smashed upon contact.

"One of the strangest things," Laura recalled, "was a clock that had belonged to my grandmother. It was a wind-up type, with a key, and it worked perfectly well in every other room in the house, but it would not keep time in that parlor. Sometimes it sped up to three times the normal speed. Mostly, it just stopped dead."

One day, after she had been in the home a while and had logged a fair share of experiences, Laura ran into the previous owner. During the casual conversation, the former resident asked, "So, have you met Philip yet?"

Laura smiled and nodded, realizing this was the name of her unseen tenant. Laura then shared some of her more colorful experiences with the seller—who, conveniently, had not thought to mention information about the phantom resident who had been included as a free-of-charge extra in Laura's house.

"I learned that the former owner's children had seen Philip in that parlor. Evidently," Laura said, "Philip had committed suicide in a second-floor bedroom and was laid out in the back parlor, the site of most of the disturbances. She also told me that Philip had been seen roaming at the top of the second-floor stairs."

Strange events continued for a short while thereafter. "But, at least now I had a name to go with the noise," Laura said, smiling in her Cecil County office and recalling her experiences from nearly two decades ago. "But, with little effort on my part," she added, "eventually, Philip was exorcised."

One day, a woman arrived at Laura's haunted home and introduced herself as Philip's daughter.

"She looked ashen and frightened," Laura recalled. "She had been having nightmares about this house where she had grown up. In her dreams, it was full of icicles, like the house in Dr. Zhivago. She said she wanted to spend some time upstairs, in her old bedroom."

Laura led her visitor through the house and up to the second floor. After two hours, she came down.

"Her face was swollen from crying," Laura remembered, "but as she left she said she felt more at peace. After that, we never heard from Philip again. Whatever he was looking for, or was concerned about, must have been settled with that visit."

I wondered if Laura had ever been scared by the disturbances.

"I never felt bad in that house," she said. "There are times when you can walk into a place and feel spirits, and the hackles rise on the back of your neck. It wasn't like that. That home was comfortable. But," she added with a smile, "I didn't appreciate it at 3 in the morning when glass was crashing.

"As I said, I do believe in the sprit world. In fact, I believe in a lot more than ghosts. I believe there's a lot more out there than we are aware of."

Miss Mischievous of Oak Spring Farm

Where to start? Should I begin this story by sharing the mysterious, middle-of-the-night footsteps my wife, Kathleen, heard in the attic during the first night of our November weekend at Oak Spring Farm? Or should I run through a litany of bizarre events that have happened at the historic inn, as told to me by Frank Harrelson, one of the present owners. I also have the option of quoting from the newspaper article—"Strange Noises Give Credence To Stories of Youngster's Ghost." Then there are the other published ghost tales about the house by reporter and former resident Lindsey Stringfellow Weilbacher.

From whichever point I start, we will eventually arrive at the same place and focus on the resident ghosts of the 1826 Virginia inn listed on the National Register of Historic Places.

I was invited by Sandy and Frank Harrelson to spend the autumn weekend in their bed and breakfast, which they had purchased in December 1997. During the stay, I was scheduled to perform two evening storytelling programs in nearby Fairfield. I would be sharing the bill with a pair of outstanding musicians, performers and Civil War historians—"The Professor and Mrs. Gibson"—actually named Pat and Keith Gibson of nearby Buena Vista, Virginia.

Sandy Harrelson had mailed me material about the scenic attractions in Rockbridge County, in the western side of the state. More importantly, she provided background about her ghosts. But, being so far away from my usual Delmarva haunts, these

Southern stories seemed distant and a bit mild, at least that's what I thought until the middle of the first evening.

Following the first show on Friday night, the entertainers and audience were invited to a reception being held on the first floor of Oak Spring Farm. As the chatter progressed and participants weaved and moseyed about, someone mentioned the word "ghosts."

Soon, those of us who remained in the old parlor past midnight were spellbound as Frank and Sandy told of the activities they and their guests had encountered and of the tales that they had been told.

Unprepared, I began taking notes on small 3 X 5 index cards, moved up to blank napkins and eventually filled a few sheets of blank paper I had found nearby. (I didn't want to leave the room and miss anything.)

Soon after the opening, Sandy said she heard small footsteps and initially thought they were just someone else in the house, except that they seemed a bit too light to be those of Frank or their daughter, Elizabeth. On other occasions, items disappeared for a time and then, unexplainably, reappeared where they were supposed to be.

One day, while in the kitchen, Sandy saw a metal pan actually fly across the room—from the sink wall to the far doorway—and just miss the top of their dog's head. However, it wasn't too much later that the pet died.

In the spring, a young boy who helped with the yard work asked, "Do you know about the ghosts?"

Frank and Sandy didn't but they soon obtained newspaper articles written by a former owner that filled in a lot of the blanks.

Miss Mischievous

In "World on A String," printed in the *Buena Vista News*, Lindsey Stringfellow Weilbacher described her experiences with ghosts while the owner of Oak Spring Farm.

"Yes, ghosts . . . . we have two in the residence with us," she wrote.

In her column, Weilbacher described experiences that her mother, Mrs. S., who also lived in the home, had shared. The older woman felt someone was sneaking up on her as she worked around the house, but when she turned quickly, no one was there.

Eventually, water faucets would be turned on, books were knocked off tables and the sound of footsteps was heard in the long hall.

Mrs. S. said, "I'm not afraid of it—there's nothing scary about it but it's so annoying. What I'd like to do is catch it and just shake it good."

Weilbacher wrote, "She sounded very much like a mother who wanted to catch a naughty child and just give it 'what for.' "

Not too many weeks later, a middle-aged woman arrived at Oak Spring Farm and said she was the granddaughter of an old couple who had owned the property until the 1950s. She was nostalgic, talking about the "old days," and Weilbacher invited the surprise visitor in. The woman remained for less than an hour, roaming the house and recalling times spent there as a child.

"Finally," Weilbacher wrote, "she got ready to leave and looked out the kitchen window towards Moores Creek. 'And that's where my little sister drowned,' she said sadly.

"My ears perked up to say the least, but I didn't mention anything about the mischievous spirit which seemed to annoy my mother so much."

The visitor explained that one day, her sister went out into the back yard and tried to get across the rain-swollen creek to get to her mother and grandmother who were in a meadow.

"She was swept off the crossing log into the creek and drowned quickly," the ghost's sister said, sadly.

After the visitor left, Weilbacher told the story to her mother and husband. The elderly woman described the ghost's antics as "annoying, like a child can be sometimes."

Weilbacher wondered if the naughty, playful ghost of the child who died in the 1930s was still trying to reach its mother or gain attention from those in the present.

The Indian

In a subsequent column, Weilbacher shared tales of the Indian ghost, who made itself known about six months after the little girl phantom first became active.

Weilbacher's husband, Ed, claimed there was a cold spot—where the main landing of the front stairs turned to the left. Weilbacher responded that it was just a draft. But, on more than one occasion, Ed said he had been tripped by an unseen force at that precise spot on the staircase.

Eventually, the second presence seemed to become a bit more bold. While watching television in the parlor, just to the left of the entry hall, Ed "stiffened and breathed softly, 'Oh, my God . . . .' "

His gaze froze toward the front doorway, where he claims to have seen a man silhouetted against the newel post of the staircase. " 'He was just standing there, with one hand on the post looking towards us,' Ed said."

After further conversation, Ed described the figure as wearing a cloak or robe, that was shapeless and hung all the way down to the floor.

That summer, the couple found a large number of arrowheads while working in the garden and they started joking about the figure, describing it as "Ed's Indian."

A few months later, a relative was sleeping with Weilbacher's daughter in what is now the Willow Room, on the second floor. The daughter was startled to see a tall figure leaning over the older woman, and the stranger later was described as wearing a long robe with feathers.

Subsequently, an archaeologist examined the arrowheads and said the location of the farm is listed as a major Indian site on Virginia state maps. Apparently, the springs at the farm attracted wandering bands of Indians and some of the arrowheads and artifacts were said to be approximately 6,500 years old.

These facts seem to indicate that there is a distinct possibility that Oak Spring Farm is built over an old Indian camping ground or gathering site.

The Present

In a July 1998 story in *The News-Gazette*, Roberta Anderson wrote, "None of the Harrelsons feel ill at ease about sharing their home with the playful spirit of the little girl. 'She's not a mean ghost, just a playful child,' Sandy Harrelson solemnly explains. Liz Harrelson has even named her 'Little Miss Mischievous.' This seems appropriate after another Harrelson daughter who was home for a visit reported having her bare feet unexplainably tickled."

One of the most interesting events was when some guests—who were at Oak Spring Farm with their two young daughters—complained during breakfast the following morning about the people staying on the third floor who were making noises throughout the night.

"They wanted us to tell them to be quiet," Frank recalled, "but there are no rooms on the third floor, only an empty, unused attic."

One time, two women were staying in the inn with their daughters, and they asked the innkeeper who was playing music during the early hours of the morning.

"My stereo wasn't working," Frank said. "It had been hit by lightning. So there was no way there could have been any music coming from anywhere inside the house. They said it sounded like old time music from the Civil War and they looked out into the meadow to see if there were campfires and soldiers out there."

At breakfast another morning, a guest asked the Harrelsons if anyone had checked in after midnight. "He said he heard people walking up and down the hall after midnight," Sandy said, "but no one checked in that late."

"There was a woman," Frank said, "who was trying to take a nap in the middle of the afternoon, and the door in the Orchard Room kept opening and closing. Annoyed, the woman said she got up from bed and turned toward the door and, for a split second, saw a little girl in the doorway. Then the ghost disappeared."

While sleeping in the Orchard Room during our stay, my wife, Kathleen, and I both heard footsteps coming from the attic above our head. Guests staying in the Maple Room also have reported footsteps above that room, apparently originating in the vacant attic.

Less frequent appearances of the Indian have occurred. After one more recent sighting of the Indian in the main entry hall, an arrowhead was found in the cellar, directly below the first floor hallway where the apparition appeared.

"I like the little girl, and I believe if she is here, she's happy," Sandy said, speaking of the young ghost. "We have a cat, dolls and toys. I'd like to think she'd be very comfortable and feel at home now. It seems that things tend to pick up around Christmastime. When else would a little girl be active?"

Frank agreed. "If there really is a ghost here who is a little girl, I think we may have made her pretty happy."

Historical notes: Built in 1826, the plantation manor-style house is located in the Shenandoah Valley, not far from Lexington, home of Virginia Military Institute. Yankee troops, under the command of Gen. David Hunter burned the original barn on the Harrelson's property during the Civil War, or War of Northern Aggression as it is sometimes called in the South. According to Frank Harrelson, Hunter was sent to burn VMI. On the way to Lexington, the Union troops noticed that the barn was being used as a blacksmith shop and destroyed it to make sure it could not be used to help the Confederates. The present red barn was rebuilt on the foundation in 1881. The Old Valley Pike, an old winding road directly in front of the inn, was used by VMI cadets in 1864 as they marched by to participate in the Battle of New Market, approximately 80 miles to the north.

Features: Within sight of the Blue Ridge Mountains and just off the Skyline Drive, the stately building with 10 adjoining acres is close to a number of historic and recreational sites. On the inn's grounds are four large gardens, a pond, an orchard with apple, cherry and pear trees. Several acres are rented to the Natural Bridge Zoo, which uses the inn's acreage to graze miniature horses, Brahmin cows and llamas.

Take a morning country walk or relax on the double-sized front porch swing. Guests are served a gourmet country breakfast, prepared by Chef Frank. Ask to see the old stone cellar and original tree trunks that were used as the building's supports.

There are four guest rooms—Willow, Orchard, Maple and Oak—with private, modern baths. The Orchard, the largest room has a Jacuzzi-type tub and a fireplace. There also are fireplaces in the Willow and Oak rooms.

One of the highlights of your stay will be listening to innkeeper Frank's tales and stories, including the family's personal knowledge and guests' experiences with the resident ghosts. The Harrelsons quickly make you feel like one of the family.

Sightings: In the Orchard Room and Willow Room. Sounds in the attic above the Maple Room and Orchard Room. On the first floor entryway, at the foot of the main stairway.

Contact: Oak Spring Farm, 5895 Borden Grant Trail, Raphine, VA 24472; telephone (540) 377-2398, 1-800-841-8813.

16 Short Sightings

Marching Soldiers
Delaware City, Delaware

Since the days before the Civil War, Delaware City has been known as a military town. Not only was Fort Delaware, located on Pea Patch Island, used as a prison camp for Confederates, but Fort DuPont—a series of coastal gun fortifications—was established right next to the south end of the town limits. Talk to some of the long-time residents and you will discover an endless stream of folktales, humorous events, local yarns and, of course, ghost stories associated with the soldiers who lived near and in the town . . . and a fair number who seem to have never left.

One winter Saturday, I met with Mel in the parlor of his home in the middle of D.C. (That's what the locals call the water village, not to be confused with the nation's capital, of course.)

A longtime resident, Mel asked that I not share his real name, because he didn't want any trouble from other locals who might not want some of the stories to get out.

For two hours, he provided a fascinating variety of historical facts and interesting tales. He said he's been told that the movement of marching soldiers still takes place in the area around Second and Madison streets and near Henry and Madison streets—and along Henry and Second streets as well.

"In the old days, around 1915," Mel said, "there was a swinging bridge that went across the old canal and connected the town with Officer's Row at Fort DuPont. Now, the thing was the train tracks stopped at a station that's gone now, but that was located behind the First Presbyterian Church. If you drive over there on the way outta town," he added, "you'll see the church and the cemetery that are still there."

Mel explained that columns of troops from Fort DuPont would head up Henry Street to the station, to pick up supplies, including coal. Sometimes, using wagons, they would march down Second Street to head back to the fort.

"There was so much traffic on those roads that the government paved them with concrete," Mel said. "They were the first two roads made of concrete in the town, so they could handle the marching and carrying of supplies. Today, they're blacktopped over.

"The kids in the town used to follow the wagons, and they say the troops would knock off pieces of coal—so the kids could gather it up and take it home. That was the only way to heat houses in those days, with a wood or coal stove."

But, even today, some believe the soldiers still march.

"I swear," he said, "I've had people in that section of town— near the Presbyterian church and on those streets—say to me, 'Hey, did you ever hear the sound of soldiers marching?' About three of four times in the last year, I've had people tell me that at night they hear sounds of soldiers marching. They don't hear voices, just the sound of marching boots. When they get up to look, there's nothing there, and the sound goes away. Then, a few months later, they hear it again."

Friendly Presence

Newark, Delaware

Marie and Paul bought an old historic building, just outside of Newark, Delaware, in 1950. It had been a stage coach stop and later served the area as a meeting place and general store.

"The shelves were still there when we moved in," Paul said, and, apparently, so was a ghost.

He explained that there was a legend that a servant, who had lived on the third floor with the maid, had hanged himself in one of the rooms. Afterward, it was said that the dead man's restless spirit roamed the house and made its presence known.

"We had quite a few experiences," Paul said. "My wife, as far as I know, is the only person who ever saw anything. She saw his black boots coming down the steps a few times. No one else saw the man, but you knew when he was around. He made his presence known."

As time passed, Marie and Paul began to refer to the ghostly gentleman as "George," in honor of George Washington.

"My wife was home alone a lot," Paul said, "and she would hear soft breathing, in and out. Whenever the presence was around, our dog would jump up in my wife's lap. That was one of the signs, and you also could feel something was around. I heard it and my children heard it, too."

But, in Paul's case, the contact went beyond the sound of breathing and a sense of something strange in the air—one night the ghost talked to him.

"I was a teacher at the time," he said, "and I was correcting papers. It was very early in the morning, around 2 a.m. I heard an old man's voice. It was very soft, very friendly and very real. It said, 'What are you doing up so late?' Well, after that I decided to go to bed.

"But, we never had a feeling that it was unfriendly. Actually, I thought he was looking after the place. On our 25th wedding anniversary, a friend read some prayers and blessed the house and put the ghost to rest."

Did he miss the presence of his unseen resident?

"I kind of did," Paul said. "I didn't get any clear indication of whether it went to rest as a result of the prayers, but it never appeared again, or made itself known. We always thought of it as a friendly presence. We were in awe, but not frightened of it.

"Even today, so many years later, it's very clear in my mind, when I was by myself and heard that voice. It's something you don't forget. I have all good memories of the place. I just recall the presence, but I can't explain it."

Factory Fantom

Wilmington, Delaware

Tony grew up in Wilmington, but he lives near Middletown now. On an early fall evening, Tony recalled an event that happened in the 1970s, while he was working the 3 to 11 shift in a Wilmington factory.

"Me and my friend, we both saw this thing, a creature," Tony said. "We were in a big room, about 40 feet by 60 feet, cleaning off printing press rollers. The first time it happened, it was standing in the middle of the shop, and we both stopped talking and looked.

"It was about 6 feet tall and kind of blue looking. It wasn't that far away, and we couldn't distinguish any kind of facial features or clothing. It was an apparition, and definitely masculine. Even though it had no distinction, I could tell it was a guy.

"We both stared at it and stopped talking for a few seconds. Then, we looked at each other and said, 'Did you see that?' and we both said, 'Yeah!' and then it was gone."

Over the next two years, the fantom appeared about 30 to 40 times, Tony said.

"Sometimes it was close and sometimes far away. But it was always the same figure. It stayed for no more than 10 seconds at the most, usually less, say 7, 8 or 9 seconds. We were the only two that saw it. After the first time, we started getting used to it. But once we became aware of it being there, it would disappear."

Eventually the two workers would wave to the fantom. When that occurred, the visitor would disappear immediately.

"It was as if it didn't like being acknowledged," Tony said. "We'd shout, 'Hi, there! How you doing?' and it would go away. We got to be friends with it. It was more interesting than fearful. It seemed to be roaming, like it was lost. But it also seemed to be paying as much attention to us as we did to him."

Tony said once the entire factory wall, the one nearest the train tracks, was vibrating terribly. He described the event as if someone was beating on the wall. But, when they went out to investigate there was no cause. There was no train, no car crash, nothing.

"I talked to my grandfather," Tony said. "We called him 'Pop,' and he said he remembered there was an old warehouse, in the building where I was working. He said it was right up near the tracks, and years ago there was a fire in the building and someone died in there."

After Tony left the job, he still kept in touch with his friend.

"He told me there were some guys who never wanted to work the 3 to 11 shift. They were that scared."

I asked Tony if he ever told anyone about what he had seen, and also asked what type of reaction he received.

"Some would give you a look or silence," he said, "and then they would say, 'I had a similar experience.' But most didn't."

Up the Back Stairway

Disturbing Dream
Wilmington, Delaware

Dolly said that when she was in her teens her family's home backed up to a cemetery. Her brother, who was alone in a room on the second floor, had a dream that there was a man standing in the middle of his room. The unwelcome visitor had his arms crossed and looked down on the teenager.

"It only happened one time," Dolly said, "but it was so real that it really scared him. He could describe the vision clearly, and I could tell that the dream had scared my brother pretty bad. From that night on, he started sleeping with a knife under his pillow."

Three weeks later, not too long after the bothersome dream, Dolly said her brother saw that very man in the neighborhood wearing the same clothing that he had on in the dream.

"We found out he was looking at a home for sale just two blocks away. Fortunately," Dolly said, "nothing happened after that, but the dream and seeing the man really bothered my brother. In fact, he slept with that knife for a very long time, and he wouldn't let his feet or arms hang out over the bed."

Civil War Angels
Chambersburg, Pennsylvania

One Saturday night, Kevin and his mother had, what he calls "an unusual, life-saving experience."

"It was in February and the weather was very cold. We were reading in the living room when we heard a loud bang," Kevin recalled. "It was like a cannon going off. It was so loud and real that it shook me in my seat. Then soon, there was another, 'BOOM!' That one was in the kitchen. The first one came from somewhere near the front door."

To add to the evening's confusion, the phone rang a few times. But, when Kevin answered, no one was on the other end of the line.

Kevin admitted that he and his mother were scared.

47

"I was very anxious, but I also was tired, so I went to bed and tried to get some rest. But, the unexplained sounds and mysterious calls still bothered me," he said.

Kevin eventually drifted off to sleep, but had a strange dream that he remembers to this day.

"I saw three Civil War soldiers," Kevin said. "I couldn't tell if they were Union or Confederate, but they definitely were military, from that period. That's very clear in my mind. They were in uniforms, with rifles, but they were inside of our house. One was in our bathroom, another by the front door and the third one in the kitchen.

"They told me they had heard my music earlier, when I was playing the piano. They said they liked the sounds and had come over to listen and had been in our home ever since."

Kevin went on to explain that the three ghostly visitors had been killed during the Civil War and they had been roaming restlessly through Gettysburg and Chambersburg for more than 130 years. On this night, in the dream, they told Kevin that they were there to protect him and his mother.

"I woke up a short time later and went downstairs to tell my mother about my dream," he said. "She had just finished watching the news, and she said there was a story about two armed men who robbed a gas station and were thought to still be in the area. Of course, they were said to be armed and dangerous."

Because Kevin's father was out of town and since they lived in a secluded rural area, Kevin and his mother did not sleep easy that particular Saturday evening.

By Monday, when Kevin's father returned home, he told his son and wife that a man, two houses up the road, had been robbed and beaten late Saturday night or early Sunday morning by a pair of masked men. The police believe that the crime was committed by the same two persons that had robbed the nearby gas station.

"I truly believe the robbers were casing our house," Kevin said. "I think the loud sounds probably drove them away. If not, they probably looked in the windows and saw our 'Civil War angels.' That's what we call them now, our Civil War angels. I think they saved our lives that night. They haven't been back, but I just know they'll be around if we're ever in trouble again."

Shut The Door
Lewes, Delaware

In an Oct. 26, 1983, article in the *Delaware Coast Press,* a short story mentions an unusual event in the Lewes [Delaware] Cannonball House, built in 1797 and struck by a British cannonball during an attack on the sea town during the War of 1812. The paper states that a volunteer, who greeted summer visitors, continually noticed that the attic door, which was securely latched, would often be open. In the fall of 1982, the volunteer said he decided to make sure the door would remain closed over the winter.

As the DCP article stated, "He put a nail in the wood, so the latch could not be lifted. You guessed it—in the spring, the door was open once again, and the nail was gone."

There He Is Again
South St. Georges, Delaware

During a meeting at the Ches Del Restaurant on a sunny afternoon, Amanda, a high school student who lived in South St. Georges, shared the contents of her research project entitled "Ghosts." The paper included information on area spirits that she had found in books and newspaper articles. Amanda also had interviewed people in her hometown and recorded several firsthand accounts of unusual activity.

"Many people see the same ghost in the same way," she said, passing her paper across the table for me to review. Talking about one of the incidents she had discovered, Amanda said there was an older lady who had lived in a large Victorian house that was located near her family home in the small canal town.

"She lived there with her brother, and he always wore dark suits and a top hat, and they say he walked with a cane," Amanda said. "He was always known to look at his pocket watch. During his lifetime, he lived in a certain room on the second floor of the house. After the lady and her brother died, at a very old age, the house was sold to a young couple from out of state.

"They moved in with their children. We became friendly. Then, after living there about a year, the wife came over to our house in the middle of the night. She was nervous and claimed that she saw a man. He was dressed in a suit with a top hat and was looking at his pocket watch. But, she said when she walked into the second-floor room where she had seen him, he disappeared."

Amanda and some of the neighbors returned to the young woman's home and they checked the entire house. When nothing was found, the search party convinced the young woman that she probably had been dreaming.

A few years later, that family moved away. Not too much later, another family moved in.

"But," Amanda said, "they moved out within the year. They said it was because they kept seeing a man in a top hat in the same room on the second floor. And, only six months later, some friends of ours moved into that house."

Amanda said her family was careful not to tell their friends about the ghostly sightings in the old Victorian. She said they didn't want to upset the new owners and, Amanda added, she and her family had never seen anything and they weren't sure that the house actually was haunted.

"Well, it wasn't too long after they moved in," Amanda said, "that the wife came over and told us about seeing the man in the top hat, looking at his watch. They saw the man on several occasions during the following year. They said each time he was standing in the same room, looking at his watch, and he slowly disappeared when they walked in."

The next time the house was sold to two single men. But, Amanda said, they only lived there for three months.

A few years later, Amanda's mother was attending a bridal shower in Wilmington.

"During the conversation," Amanda said, "someone mentioned South St. Georges to my mother. Then, another lady sitting nearby, said, 'My brother used to live there with his friend, but they moved out because of the ghosts.'

"My mother asked several questions, and the woman replied, 'The ghost was a tall man in a top hat with a pocket watch. And he always appeared in the same room on the second floor.'

"The last I heard," Amanda added, "the house is occupied by a family with several young children. But, we don't want to tell them any of these stories because we might cause them to move out. There's no sense stirring things up for no good reason."

Missing Their Ghosts
Tangier Island, Virginia

My friend Ruth sent me this story in the mail. I figure it's best to let her tell it her way, just as it was written.

"My sister Stella and I went to Tangier Island on the cruise boat last summer. While we were there, my brother Thomas said, 'Ruth, my family hasn't seen or heard any ghosts for about six months. I think they have left us.' Then he said, 'We miss them.'

"And then things started to happen. The TV changed channels. The lights started going on and off. It did this for about 10 minutes.

"When my brother and his wife went to bed, two forms were floating over their bed. My brother said, 'That's enough!' and they disappeared.

"When his son Tommy came home that night, we told him what happened. He went up to bed and the lights upstairs went on and off for about five minutes. Tommy got up during the night to go to the bathroom, there were two forms that looked like Indians at the foot of his bed.

"My brother said I brought them back. I said, 'I think they came back when you said your family missed them.' "

Hexed Oyster Shells
Bay Vista, Sussex County, Delaware

I recalled a conversation I had a few years back with Ed, a friend of mine and an old neighbor from the Hedgeville section of Wilmington. A quick telephone call over the Christmas holidays refreshed his memory and provided an interesting story that happened in the early 1990s in Bay Vista, near the Delaware seashore resorts.

The community of about 200 homes is located west of Dewey Beach, across the manmade Lewes and Rehoboth Canal that connects the Rehoboth Bay with the Delaware Bay.

About five years ago, Ed said, there was a home in Bay Vista that was having a water and sewer line installed. The backhoe operator dug down and started bringing up oyster shells. But they were quite a bit different than the ones you find today.

"I'm telling you, Eddie," Ed said to me, "I've seen oyster shells, but I've never seen anything like these. They were 12 inches long, the largest I've ever seen or heard of."

As the construction worker continued to make a pile of shells off the side of the road, he noticed that he was bringing up things that looked like bones.

He called the Delaware State Police, who arrived and said they thought some of the debris looked like human bones. The state archaeologist arrived next and shut down the site and stopped the construction.

"Apparently," Ed said, "the backhoe had ripped into an old Indian burial site. But that wasn't a surprise, since Thompson Island, where the state controls an Indian burial ground, is right across the canal from Bay Vista. But, the strange thing is, the backhoe operator decided to take one of the shells as a souvenir, and he tossed it in the back of his pickup.

"That very same day," Ed said, "the guy had four flat tires. Later, figuring it was some kind of bad luck to take the shell from the gravesite, he brought the oyster shell back and returned it to the pile."

Ed, whose mother owns a home two blocks away in Bay Vista, spent a few days hanging around the site, watching the state archaeologist and trying to find out what was going on.

"As best as I can remember," he said, "I think they discovered three adults, two children and a dog down there. So it turned out to be an Indian burial ground after all. I remember going out with my son and finding arrowheads all around the area. It used to be farmland, and they say the Indians would use the area for camping and hunting and fishing. I don't know if you could say for sure that there was a curse on taking that shell, but that guy thought so. He told me that's why he brought it back the very next day."

Road Roamer
Elkton, Maryland

The bold headline in the *Cecil Whig* on Aug. 4, 1933, asked: "Have You Seen The Honest-To-Goodness Ghost on Phila. Road?"

Thanks to Michael Dixon of Elkton, who is an historian at the Historical Society of Cecil County, copies of two associated newspaper articles on this topic were delivered to my attention.

In the above-noted story, the anonymous newspaper writer reported:

"For those who have faith in the theory that spirits of the dead rise again and walk at night, a current story should provide a wealth of material for the imagination. It is reported—and, for that matter, from not . . . unreliable sources—that a 'ghost' has been seen walking along the Philadelphia-Baltimore highway through this section."

The story goes on to describe a "shabby, stooped man of perhaps 40 years, walking at a slow, weary pace, with a look of sadness and resignation upon his countenance. His gaze, it is said, is fixed straight ahead and he is apparently oblivious of passing automobiles."

The story was published first in Baltimore after reports by "late-traveling motorists."

The fantom, it was said, confined his activities to the same area, on U.S. Route 40, and always appeared to be walking in a northerly direction.

The first reported sighting was given by Louis L. Erhardt, a general manager of a Persian rug importing house in New York City, who stopped at a local Maryland hotel.

"Erhardt claims to have encountered the specter near the top of Bacon Hill, between North East and Elkton," the paper stated.

The salesman reported that his automobile lights "picked up the figure of the pedestrian as he was ascending the long grade. Because of the apparent weariness of the stranger, the driver paid particular attention to his progress, but found that no matter at what speed he drove, the fantom remained just within the rays of the headlights. Nevertheless, Erhardt claims, the figure had the appearance of proceeding at a slow fatigued gait.

"Truck drivers who also allege to have seen the ghost near Elkton say that he carries a pack upon his shoulder, but never asks for a ride, and that he appears and disappears suddenly out of, and again into, the shadows. Sometimes he has been encountered just out of Baltimore, sometimes on the long, isolated stretch beyond Aberdeen, and again on the lonely hills between Perryville and Elkton."

One week later, the ghost story continued, with the *Cecil Whig* announcing: "Highway Ghost Leaves Route 40 For Perryville-Port Road."

The article stated: "Maryland's highway ghost has forsaken its native Philadelphia road. First reported near Baltimore, later in the vicinity of Aberdeen, and last week said to have been seen between North East and Elkton—but always proceeding in a northerly direction on U.S. Route 40—the apparition has now digressed from its native haunts and was seen on Tuesday on the highway between Perryville and Port Deposit."

The story referred to Layton Schmidt's sighting, while he was returning to his home in Lancaster, Pennsylvania, from Baltimore through Havre de Grace.

He alleged to have seen "the specter in one of the lonely hollows near Cokesbury. Like other accounts of the ghost's escapades, Mr. Schmidt tells that during the early morning hours his car picked up the figure of a shabby, stooped old man walking slowly ahead."

Apparently, Mr. Schmidt was "badly frightened" and reported an "incoherent story" when he arrived in Rising Sun, soon after the sighting of the apparition.

According to the *Whig* article, "Traveling at a rapid rate of speed, Mr. Schmidt avers that he did not doze at the wheel, and like others who have seen the ghost, claims that the figure of the weird pedestrian remained before him in the highway for several hundred yards before it disappeared into space."

Let Me In

Gibbstown, New Jersey

John and Elaine lived in a home on the family farm. The property had been owned by the family for at least three generations. Ages ago, American Indians must have lived at the site, for they were forever finding arrowheads.

Elaine first noticed that the TV would go on in the living room for no good reason. The radio also seemed to have a mind of its own, broadcasting the news and music at will. The lights were burning when she was sure she had turned them off, too. Then, the cellar door would be open, even though it had been closed and latched, she was sure.

"I thought my husband had left it open, or didn't think to shut off the lights or the TV," Elaine said. "But, then, in the middle of the night both showers would turn on."

"About this time, we were getting concerned," John said. "It wasn't just the lights and the door, but the shower, too. And I was saying this was impossible, but it was happening."

"We'd go out and come home," Elaine said, "and all the lights would be on and the doors would be open. It wasn't safe. This was getting serious. We even put in dead bolts, but the door was still wide open, and neither of us had done it."

After the death of Elaine's father, her mother was living with them for a while and she wouldn't let her granddaughter—Elaine's daughter—go into the basement.

"She said there were ghosts and bad spirits down there," John said. "I wondered if she had had any experiences in our house? In fact, our daughter would go to the top of the cellar steps and start screaming, 'Nanny said it's bad down there!' We never discovered why she said it, but it was a little unnerving."

One day, Elaine saw her father's ghost walking down the hall and go into the dining room.

Soon afterwards, there was repeated knocking at the front door, but each time they checked there was no one there.

Elaine and John thought it was the neighborhood children, playing games. But they could see clearly out the large glass panels and there was no one in sight when the knocking occurred.

"Then the doorbell started," John said. "I could stand on the front step and see the doorbell depressing and releasing. It was definitely not kids, I could see it being activated—going in and out—and nobody was there. Someone was ringing it, but no one was there—no one that I could see.

"About the same time there was a murder in the area. A young girl was picked up as she was coming home from a dance. She was killed only blocks from the house. The killer backed over her with a pickup truck. After that, the dead girl was spotted walking and hitchhiking by men leaving work from a nearby refinery."

A neighbor of the couple stopped and picked the girl up.

"He said he had kids of his own," John said. "It was at night and he said when she got into the cab she didn't speak. Then, at the end of the ride he turned and she wasn't there. This type of thing went on for about a year, along with all the other stuff."

During a trip to Florida a few months later, Elaine was visiting her aunt.

"I remember that she said, 'Oh, you're like me.' My aunt explained," Elaine added, "that souls need a place to come and that's what I am. They come to me. The little girl was coming to my house to seek safety. My aunt told me to find a priest. He came and said we probably had a poltergeist and he blessed the house and everything disappeared.

"I remember when he came to our front door. He stopped and said, 'I feel it. Don't get involved with it. It's here.' He went to every room, including the basement. He used holy water and incense and read a prayer. Then, everything disappeared."

Was it a big change?

John smiled. "You still wake up and wonder: Is the shower going to come on? Is the door going to open? You keep expecting it. You wonder if it's really going to work. But, thankfully, it did."

The couple later discovered that the family property had been the site of an Indian village and burial ground. They believe that could have contributed to the activities they experienced.

"Whatever it was, a ghost, dead Indians, a poltergeist, we'll never know. But," John said, smiling, "I'll tell you this, it made a believer of me when I watched that doorbell button going in and out."

Trying To Get Home
Sussex County, Delaware

An often told story in the Delaware resort area involves the ghost of an elderly woman that haunts one of the shopping centers located on the main highway between Lewes and Dewey Beach.

As the story goes, many years ago—before the days of outlets, wall-to-wall fast food joints and bumper-to-bumper traffic—

an old farmhouse stood on some very desirable real estate that was perfect for a shopping center. Real estate agents and developers kept approaching the old woman, but she wouldn't accept their offers and refused to sell her homestead.

It's said the woman had a problem with her vision. Although she wasn't blind, her eyesight was very poor. To help her get to the mailbox and back, a rope was tied from the porch of the farmhouse to the end of the country lane so she could maneuver her way along the lengthy driveway.

One winter during a snowstorm, the woman fell into the snow while returning from the mailbox. No one knows if she lost hold of the rope, if her guideline broke or if it became too difficult to handle in the wind and snow. Unable to rise, she remained on the ground and was covered by deadly layers of snow and ice—and she passed away alone, in the bitter cold during that winter storm.

Eventually, her home and property were sold, and a department store, discount house or strip mall—I've never been able to find out the exact site—was built over the spot where she had died.

In recent years, people claim the old woman's ghost has been sighted in the large store and in some of the smaller shops in this particular shopping center.

Perhaps she is seeking the other end of her lifeline, hoping it will lead her to a place of eternal rest.

Restless Resident
Wilmington, Delaware

Jane's home was built in the late 1940s or early 1950s. It is located in an older development outside Wilmington, not far from busy Route 202. The tree-lined streets and neatly kept residences remind passersby of the neighborhood where Ward and June Cleaver brought up young Wally and the Beaver.

But, in the case of this house, that's where the similarity ends.

Since her husband traveled five days a week, Jane spent a lot of time at home alone. The couple had moved into their two-story home in the late 1980s, and they lived there about 10 years.

"The first time something out of the ordinary happened," Jane recalled, "I was ironing in the family room. I heard what sounded like thundering, running feet over my head. I tried to identify the sound and thought there might be a squirrel, an opossum or some other animal on the roof—or maybe even in the attic space over the family room."

Grabbing a flashlight, she ran upstairs, opened the door that led to the attic and found nothing at all.

"There was nothing that I could see," she said, "so I wrote it off to the heavy truck traffic on nearby Route 202. But, I heard the same running feet thumping over my head about a month later. This time I told my husband about it, and he told me I was crazy."

Smiling, Jane admitted that she started thinking she, indeed, might be going out of her mind. But, a short time passed and, in the middle of the night, she was awakened by her dog, who slept at the foot of her bed.

"He was standing at the closed bedroom door growling a low, throaty growl with his ears flattened and hackles raised. He was a big dog," she added, "and a great watch dog. So I opened the door and let him go, thinking there must be a prowler outside. I knew the dog, with his vicious barking, would scare anyone away."

With a phone in one hand and a 12-gauge shotgun on her lap, Jane waited. Eventually, she left her room and headed downstairs. She discovered her dog barking toward the laundry room.

"I didn't hear any suspicious sounds, so I carefully checked the room. There was nothing there."

After that, the running sounds continued once every few months. Jane's husband never heard them—until one night.

"We had just gone to bed and were almost asleep," she said, recalling the night when he became a believer. "Suddenly, we both were raised out of bed by the sound of VERY LOUD running feet that sounded like someone had jumped from tree branches hanging over our roof. It sounded like it was right above our heads. My husband flew out of bed and ran downstairs, thinking there was someone on our roof. It was that loud. When he found nothing, I finally got to say, 'I told you I wasn't crazy!' "

Things eventually settled down, and there were no more strange sounds until some friends stayed at the house for a few days.

"I think I would have dismissed all of the unusual happenings," Jane said, "were it not for our friends, who did some dog sitting in the house while we went away. They stayed in our guest room, which was right behind our bedroom. When we returned, we asked them how everything went, and if they had a comfortable stay.

"They both responded by demanding to know 'what the hell is in your house?' I asked what they meant, and they told us they had heard pounding noises or thumping sounds, as if someone were running over their heads. It was then that I knew for certain that there definitely was something out of the ordinary going on in the house.

"We eventually named the ghost," Jane said. "We called him 'Herb.' I often wonder if the family who bought the house from us have ever heard of 'Herb' the ghost. But, I'm not about to go up and knock on the door and ask."

Good idea.

Bring It Back!
North East, Maryland

Marjorie had decided to give her great-granddaughter, Ashley, a special locket that had been given to Marjorie by her late husband. One afternoon, she took the gold chain and ornate oval piece from its special compartment in the jewelry box and placed it in the middle of her bed. She left the room for a few minutes, to select a photograph she planned to place inside the locket—so it would serve as a reminder to Ashley of her great grandparents.

When Marjorie returned, the locket was gone.

She looked all over the room—on the bedspread, under the bed, inside the jewelry box and beneath the furniture. But, somehow the locket had just seemed to disappear.

A few weeks later, Marjorie and her granddaughter, Debbie, visited me at a book signing in North East, Maryland, at England's Colony On The Bay. During the conversation, Debbie mentioned the disappearance of the locket and Marjorie told me the story.

I suggested to Marjorie that she go back into her room and ask out loud for the ghost to bring it back.

"Well, I guess I have nothing to lose," Marjorie replied.

Within the week, I received an e-mail note from Debbie, stating simply, "The locket is back."

I called Marjorie and she said, "I went back into the bedroom and said, 'Bring my locket back. I want to give it to our great

59

granddaughter!' A couple of days later, I found it inside my jewelry box, in the compartment where it belonged. I know I left it on the bed, and I don't know how it got back in there. But, asking for it worked. I said, 'Thanks.' I'm still sort of surprised when I think about it, but it worked anyway."

House For Sale

Hockessin, Delaware

Bernadette and her husband followed their real estate agent as she entered an empty home in Hockessin—through the back door.

"I thought it was a little strange that we went in through the back entrance," Bernadette said, "but, we just followed along as the agent conducted the tour. The other odd thing was that she entered every room except the living room. When we got to that point, she pointed to the room and we went inside and looked around ourselves.

"Also, the agent had a friend with her. They had been waiting for us in the driveway when we arrived. At first, I didn't think anything of these oddities. But, later I understood."

As Bernadette and her husband left the living room, she noticed a "ghost" or "apparition" of another, older woman.

"I didn't say anything," Bernadette said. "I just kept walking, but the ghost followed us through the entire house. It was as if she were serving as an escort, showing us around."

When the interior tour was completed, the agent asked Bernadette what she thought of the home.

"I asked the agents how long ago the woman who had lived there had died? And they were astonished. They immediately asked, 'Who told you?' I said I saw the woman as we went through the rooms. They didn't say anything, and we didn't buy the house.

"It didn't bother me. It wasn't frightening," she added. "I had the sense that the ghost was trying to let us know that it was a very beautiful house. In fact, I sensed that she was proud of it and wanted to have someone who would take care of it move in."

Bernadette said this occurred about 10 years ago, and occasionally she's been tempted to revisit the home and ask about the ghost. But she never followed through on the idea.

Amazing Coincidence?
Washington, D.C.

Suzette is an antique dealer with shops in Annapolis and two other Maryland cities. While she's only been in the business since 1993, an event that occurred 11 years ago turned out to be quite an amazing coincidence, or perhaps it was the work of fate. You decide.

In 1987, her husband, a Washington, D.C., police officer was walking his beat. Passing a house that was being renovated, he got into a conversation with a worker who, for some unknown reason, gave the officer a few old postcards. When he came home, he passed them on to his wife, Suzette. She found them interesting and placed the antique postcards inside a box in which she kept special mementos.

When she opened her antique business five years ago, Suzette was talking to a lady in the shop and, for the first time since she had received them, pulled out the six old postcards.

"Being in the business by that time," she said, "I suddenly realized that they were actual picture post cards. That means they were real photographs of people that were made to be sent through the mail. I figured they were worth about $35 each, and was really impressed. I was having tea with the woman and was planning to sell them if I got a good price."

Later, while talking to her mother, Suzette took out the post-cards and told her mother about their value.

"As she looked at them," Suzette said, "my mother got a strange look on her face. She asked me, 'Where did you say you got these?' And I explained that they were given to my husband several years ago in Washington. Then she asked me, 'Do you know who this is?' I said I had no idea. It turned out that it was my great-great-grandmother's son, at his training camp in Pennsylvania during World War I."

Suzette said the card had been sent from Pennsylvania to her great-great-grandmother's address. There was a message on the back, written and dated 1917—80 years before the cards were given to Suzette's husband by a total stranger. On the front was a picture of about 20 men in the unit, a dog mascot and the unit's cook. Her relative's head was circled, and there was an arrow pointing to him.

"There's no way now that I would sell them in a hundred years," Suzette said. "People in the family ask, 'Who gave these to you?' They can't believe it was just a coincidence that they came into my possession. In a way, neither can I. It's like I was supposed to get them."

Ghost of Fiddler's Bridge

Progress has just about wiped out old Scott Run. Remnants of the small stream still trickle on the south side of the Chesapeake and Delaware Canal, not too far below the southern section of the village of St. Georges, Delaware. But, locals say the creek is nothing like it was more than 180 years ago, when the fiddler's story is believed to have happened.

The particular area where the legend took place was pretty much destroyed when the first St. Georges Bridge—a steep, two-lane span—was erected more than 50 years ago. Today, the newest bridge—a modern, multi-lane superspan that stretches over the canal within shouting distance of the old elevated structure—is an important part of new Route 1.

This engineering marvel, created in 1997 in the name of progress, is designed to deliver beachbound motorists to their weekend destinations more quickly. In doing so, the new structure has contributed to the death of the old stream's natural beauty and it also takes travelers farther away from what's left of Scott Run, the legendary site of one of New Castle County's most interesting folktales.

I had heard about the story of the Fiddler's Bridge from locals in Port Penn and from others who had asked about it over the years. Fortunately, I met a woman, who knew an older man who said he would share his experience at the bridge, but only if I swore to never reveal his name.

I agreed and, after a few phone calls, we agreed to meet for breakfast at the ChesDel Restaurant, a well-known family dining spot on Route 13, south of St. Georges and west of Port Penn.

Originally, the ChesDel was made of two diners from the city of Wilmington that had been saved by the owner and moved to the site. Today, a large dining room has been added in the back, but the main entrance is through the stainless steel diner, and that's where Jessie and I had breakfast.

Jessie isn't his real name. I had to change it so no one would be able to identify him. But, he looks like a Jessie, so that identification seems to fit. He told me to say he was from Port Penn, but that's not true either. I can't reveal the exact town where he lives, but it is located in the Delaware portion of Delmarva, and below the canal.

According to Jessie, he worked his entire life as a farmer and also spent a good number of seasons trapping muskrat and beaver in the local marshes for other farmers who, as he said, "needed crop management of their untamed animal population."

The pelts paid well, and he said he made a good living. At 75 years of age, Jessie told me he enjoys recalling some of the stories he was told during his early years. In those days, when there was only radio for entertainment, his father and grandfather would fill his young mind with tales of pirates in the marshes, gold in the ground, witches in the woods and monsters behind every tree and bush, especially when it was dark.

They lived out in the country, and that made the scary stories seem even more real.

"I tell you," Jessie said, taking a drag on his Camel and lifting his coffee cup, "I sure wasn't eager to go out in the woods, even in daytime, hearing some of those tales. To be honest," Jessie said, his voice a little lower, "there were some nights I didn't even go to the outhouse. I held it all night through 'cause I was so fearful. Unless the house was up in flames, I wasn't going out nowhere alone."

Smiling at the memories, Jessie lowered his voice, looked up across the table and said, "Look here. The reason I don't want you to use my real name is 'cause of my wife. She got religion a while back."

I nodded and smiled. I knew what was coming, had heard it a dozen times before, but I waited for Jessie to share the reason himself.

"I go with her to hear the preacher, sometimes, but not that often. She says her church don't believe in ghosts. Says they're the devil in disguise. Tells me that she don't wanna hear no talk about them—no how. But I do what I want to do, scare the grand-kids to hell and back when she and my daughter ain't around. But, outta respect for my wife—she's a good woman to put up with me all these long years—I don't wanna cause her no needless embar-rassment. So, that's why I don't want my name used. But," Jessie paused and smiled, "I bet half the women in her church would read the book in secret and not tell nobody about it."

I agreed and reassured him that he wasn't the first to offer me his explanation. It made him feel better when I told him about the preachers and priests who had passed tales along and who also wanted to remain anonymous.

Pleased to be included in such fine company, he began to offer a number of area yarns, starting off with a description of the black, horsedrawn hearse in the Blackbird Forest. "The horses are ink black, with red eyes and silver bridles. When steam escapes from their noses you can see the black and red death plumes standing up over their heads. They don't make no noise when they come by, like their hooves are floatin' and don't touch the ground. The hearse has glass on all sides and an invisible driver, but inside are bodies, dozens of 'em, with their chalk white faces pressed against the inside of the glass, an' their hands are clawin' to get out and go among the livin'. They say if you see that funeral wagon while you're out there huntin', it's best to go in the other direction real fast. 'Cause if it decides to stop for you, you won't be going home for supper."

As Jessie leaned back to let the waitress clear our empty breakfast plates, he took off his volunteer fireman's baseball cap, rubbed his white hair and stretched his arms out across the back of the dark blue, leather booth.

After a brief mention about ghosts of drowning victims and bridge workers in the C & D Canal, he told me of restless spirits he'd seen in a few local graveyards—while he was working as a gravedigger to make some extra money. But, those are stories for another time. On this day, the conversation eventually turned to the topic of our meeting, the Ghost of Fiddler's Bridge.

"I tell you, there's lots of stories," Jessie said, his eyes looking toward the ceiling, "but, that fiddler up the road is one of the best."

Looking out the window, Jessie turned to his rear and pointed north, up Route 13. "You go up about a mile," he said, "then take the lane to the old bridge. Not that new one, the old one," he stressed. "Just before you start to hit the ramp, look off to the right. You'll see the green sign with white letters. Says 'Scott Run.' That's the spot, or what's left of it, where they say that old fiddler used to play."

"Does he still play?" I asked.

"Hell, I don't know. But if he did, who could hear him now. They done took his wooden bridge away with the first big bridge. Now, with that second one, goin' over the canal right next to the first, they just about wiped out his stream. If he's still playin', I bet it ain't no happy tune no more. I'd say it's gotta be funeral music, 'cause he can't be happy about the way the area's been torn up. Killed a lot of nature, it has."

The legend has been written up in area newspapers for some years, and told by word of mouth long before that.

It's said that Oscar, that's what name Jessie calls the fiddler, was a slave who was not the greatest worker. He liked to whistle and sing while he did as little work as possible, just enough to get by. But, at night, back in the slave quarters, he would play tunes on the fiddle all night long. They were fast tunes for dancing and slow tunes for singing. If anybody wanted to hear a good song, all they had to do was go over to Oscar's and ask. The fiddler would play for free and all night long, for he loved to make music and make people happy.

As time went on, and Oscar's fiddling became more well known, blacks and whites, slaves and free would head for his shack to be entertained and hear him perform.

The overseer, who was in charge of the slave work detail, was not pleased with Oscar's fame. He also did not approve of the fiddler doing little work during the day and saving his energy to play all night.

"One day," said Jessie, "the boss man, he beat the crap outta Oscar. They say he beat him so bad the other slaves had to carry him back to his shack. The next morning, he was too sick to work, so the overseer tossed Oscar out of his house and the fiddling slave had to go and live in the woods.

"My granddaddy said Oscar built a shack back there, far into the woods and would just play the fiddle all day and all night. There was just woods and farmland around here then, and the sound would travel all through the woods. People would know that Oscar was still alive and out there. After some time, they would leave food—pieces of fruit, cake and pies, pieces of bread, anything they didn't want or had extra of—out on their steps during the day, while they were out workin'. They say Oscar came by and picked it up and took it back to his shack to eat.

"As the years went by," Jessie added, "people in carriages and on horses passing the wooden bridge that used to go over Scott Run, they would see Oscar, this crazy fiddler there and they'd throw him coins and he'd play them a little tune."

There are two versions of what happened to Oscar. In one story, the fiddler went crazy, or was drunk, fell off the bridge and drowned in the rushing water of the creek below the bridge.

The other tale says Oscar just grew old like everyone else and died. But, his fiddling still can be heard near the site of the long gone wooden bridge.

"I only heard the story about him drownin' in the creek," Jessie said. "I like to think that's what happened. That would make him more of a ghost, from my point of view. You know, accidental death and all."

According to other sources, the fiddler would continue to play, even after his death, especially if someone stopped at night and tossed silver dollars into the stream below the bridge. In one case, it's said the passersby didn't only get music. One dark night, Oscar himself rose up out of the water, playing the fiddle and floating up toward the road. That sent the drunken partygoers heading for the high ground.

"I remember talk, when I was a kid, about people sayin' they knew people who would throw money, small coins, into the water as they passed over the bridge at night—hopin' to hear some music from Oscar."

"Any luck?" I asked.

"Not that I know of, but they were probably cheap. If the ghost wants silver dollars, then you gotta give him silver dollars. Now, who do you know is gonna stand on Route 13 near the St. Georges Bridge and part with a real silver dollar today? First, they'd probably get runned over by a passin' semi, or they'd get locked up and put away for tossin' good money after bad.

"I ain't sayin' Oscar ain't still there, somewhere," Jessie said, holding up his hands, "but, don't you think he's probably moved on to nicer and quieter surroundings? If I was a ghost and they took my haunted spot away, you'd find me in a nice, out-of-the-way graveyard where they would appreciate me more and you could hear my fiddle music a whole lot better."

Author's note: To locate the remnants of Scott Run, head north on Route 13, approximately 7/10 of a mile from the ChesDel Restaurant and take the road leading toward the old St. Georges Bridge. Pull onto the northbound shoulder. You will see Scott Run, a small stream flowing below. It also is marked by a green-and-white road sign on the ramp—slightly to the west—leading north onto the newer Route 1 bridge over the canal. But, it is to the east—toward the Delaware River, along the small, overgrown creek—that Oscar would play his fiddle.

And maybe he still does . . . for the right price.

Ticking Tomb

This is one of the most well-known and favorite legends of the northern Delmarva Peninsula, and it is one I have used for many years during my storytelling programs. A Mid-Atlantic folktale, it has been handed down through both pen and word of mouth for more than 200 years, since the days after the American Revolution. It is especially unique since it takes place in three adjoining states—Pennsylvania, Maryland and Delaware, and each colony proudly claims a portion of the story as its own. More importantly, there are many who have located this hallowed site and swear they have heard its mysterious message, especially during late evening graveyard visits.

I n southeast Pennsylvania, in the London Tract "Hardshell" Baptist graveyard—near the narrow curves along the banks of the White Clay Creek—there's a special tombstone with a distinctive name. In the immediate area, it's known as "Ticky Tomb" or the "Ticking Tomb" and, less frequently, the "Ticking Stone."

The site is not far off Route 896, a two-lane, country road that winds through Delaware and up into the Keystone State. Follow these directions and you will find the gravesite you seek.

Go north, past the Delaware line. Continue through a very short sliver of the road that belongs to Maryland, the Free State. After you enter the state of Pennsylvania, designated by the large "welcome" sign, travel only 3/4 of a mile. Turn right onto South Bank Road; it's marked with a green road sign. Follow this road's winding curves for about a mile and a half as it leads down to the bottom of a steep hill.

Enter the church graveyard through the white, wooden gate. The tomb you seek is located in this ancient boneyard of departed souls that surrounds a small one-room, gray stone church. The entire area is enclosed by a stone wall, remortared in some areas and crumbling away in others.

Many of the tombstones are leaning over. A good many are illegible, their surfaces almost totally smooth.

The elements and weather of more than 200 cycles of the four seasons—the heavy rains, chipping frost and baking heat—have slowly and silently done their work. Hand-chiseled carvings that gave clues to the history of the churchyard's permanent residents have been obliterated, long lost to the memories of those resting beneath the ground.

But, if you know which stone to visit, and just the right way to approach the silent slab, you can place your ear beside the green moss and pitted rock and listen . . . and hear . . . the steady "tick—tick—tick"—of the Ticking Tomb.

Some say the sound is the steady plea of the broken heart of a lover who had lost a mate.

Others believe, with equal fervor, it is the rhythmic pulse of a watch, an ancient timepiece, that rests—but still beats—within the vest of the entombed.

Skeptics of the unknown argue that it must be an underground stream or nest of some family of varmints that causes the noise.

Think what you may.

To find the real answer, we must travel into history and visit the past. Our destination is 1764, 235 years ago, when two well-respected surveyors—Charles Mason and Jeremiah Dixon—were working within two miles of the mysterious site of the present day Ticking Tomb.

The whole reason for drawing the famous Mason-Dixon line was because the Calverts of Maryland and the Penns of Pennsylvania and Delaware didn't know exactly what they owned. And the people who lived in the border areas of the three colonies didn't know where, or to whom, they belonged.

For many years, residents of towns like Rising Sun, Maryland, and Oxford, Pennsylvania, were paying taxes to both the Catholic Calverts and Quaker Penns.

To be honest, the Calverts and the Penns didn't care as long as they got their taxes; and the people couldn't do anything about it, so they paid twice and kept quiet. But the dilemma really caught the attention of the Penn family when sea captains, who came up the Delaware River to pick up and deliver supplies, told the Philadelphians that, according to their navigational instruments, their prosperous City of Brotherly Love was located in the province of Maryland.

This got the attention of the authorities, and soon representatives of the two bickering colonies went to London to resolve the problem. In 1760, an agreement was signed, and Mason and Dixon were contracted to draw an accurate boundary. The two men arrived on Philadelphia's cobblestoned streets in 1763.

By 1764, the solitude of the region around Newark, Delaware, and the Head of Elk (Elkton), Maryland, was broken as the two surveyors arrived. They were accompanied by a large party consisting of chain bearers, rod men, ax-men, cooks, baggage handlers, Indian scouts and camp followers. For a short time, while work was occurring on the area known as The Wedge, the two surveyors bedded down at the old St. Patrick's Inn, that was located just east of the present day Deer Park Tavern on Main Street in Newark.

It's said, for entertainment, Mason and Dixon had brought along a pet bear.

Soon, a tent city had formed.consisting of a ragtag assembly of pack mules and their handlers, gypsies and fiddlers, plus an assortment of peddlers, pickpockets and preachers. Many would eventually travel the length of the Maryland-Pennsylvania border and leave their markers—for more than 330 miles. But before the historic journey would begin, an unusual event occurred.

Charles Mason was a Anglican and a member of the Royal Observatory of Greenwich England. It's said he was of refined upbringing and that he possessed a serious scientific spirit. His colleagues described him as a "serious, methodical man, lacking in humor but competent and devoted to his assigned tasks."

On the opposite end of the personality spectrum was Jeremiah Dixon. A bachelor Quaker and the son of an English coal miner, Dixon was noted for his impulsive spirit, steady courage, speed with details and worldly street-wise savvy.

The two men created an unusual pair, but they got along well and accomplished their work with painstaking attention to detail.

Several years earlier, the famous scientist Sir Isaac Newton had convinced the British government that there was a need for an accurate, portable, chronometer—a time piece—that could be used at sea to determine both time and longitude.

In 1714, the British Parliament had announced a reward of 20,000 pounds for a chronometer-like invention. For half a century, the greatest minds on the Continent and in the British Isles were at work on an invention that would insure international fame and a very rich reward. Among the notables in the running was Charles Mason.

At the moment that particularly interests us, the surveyors were working in tents, not far from the present day town of Landenberg, Pennsylvania. Scouts had returned with supplies from nearby Maryland and Newark, and Mason was at work on a version of the chronometer, an important project to which he had devoted many years of effort and continued to fine tune during his survey work in the New World.

On this particular day, a fishwoman from the town known as the Head of Elk, a small village a few hours hike from the site of the camp, had arrived. She planned to sell her freshly caught wares to the hungry members of the survey party. The size of her obese body seemed to pale in comparison to the strength of the foul smell of the catch she had brought with her. Following along at her side was the filthiest, ugliest, fattest babe one had ever seen.

The grotesque child, named Fithian Minuit, was know in the counties of Chester, Cecil and New Castle for his huge insatiable appetite and unpleasant, dirty appearance. The young scamp was also known to devour anything—be it animal, vegetable or even mineral—that passed before his bright red, chubby cheeks.

Mason's attention was pulled from his invention to the sound of the mother, outside the tent shouting, "Fresh fish for sale! Fresh food for the surveyors! Fat and full cut shad! Crabs for the steaming!"

Responding to the woman's plea, Mason left his tent to look at the fishwoman's catch. While negotiating price, her monster child crawled into the surveyor's tent. Mason's assistant noticed the child and picked it up off the ground. Suddenly, for no reason, wee fat Fithian began to cry, then scream, then shout and, finally, beat the assistant across the chest.

Becoming nervous, the assistant surveyor picked up a small metallic object that Mason had been working on. Hoping the sight of a tiny, bright, sparkling object might amuse and quiet the child, the assistant waved Mason's invention, a small ticking sphere, in front of the unruly child.

At that moment, the fat child, thinking it was something new to eat, reached out his hands. Unfortunately, the assistant let the invention fall well within the child's grasp, and, in the flash of a regretful moment, the child had opened its mouth, shoved in the small metal object and swallowed Mason's timepiece.

Frantic with fear, the assistant tried to retrieve the precious invention from Fithian's clenched mouth. But luck had deserted the poor assistant, and it did not intend to return that day. Within seconds, Fithian was being held upside down by his foot and, at the same time, was being pounded on the back by the terrified assistant—who was demanding the return of his master's ticking globe and most valuable and precious invention.

Responding to the confusion, the surveyor and fishwife entered the tent.

"My baby!" cried the mother, who saw the swollen cheeks and blue color of Fithian's chubby face.

"My chronometer!" shouted Mason, who read the look of helpless terror on his assistant's face.

Taking control of her smiling child, the mother swung Fithian back and forth, like an oversized pendulum, while Mason's worried assistant continued to beat on the baby's back.

Dixon, who had entered the tent in the midst of the bedlam, was anything but calm. When he discovered what had occurred, his reaction was a combination of laughter and relief.

"Finally," he said, "we can be done with this nonsense of the invention and direct all of our attention to the survey!"

Mason, emotionally exhausted and weak from the realization of his loss, fell into a chair and held his face in his hands. But his expression was one of pity, not anger. Pity, not only for the years of work that had been lost, but for the ignorance of his associate who did not understand the significance of his personal disaster.

Sadly, Mason looked at those in his tent—the mother, baby, his assistant and partner Dixon. The sick surveyor picked up a half-filled bottle of dark red wine, poured himself a full glass of the liquid, and raised a toast to the small, filthy, monstrous child.

With goblet raised, Mason said, "May this fishwoman's child have a long life, and keep my invention safe within him for the rest of his days and beyond."

That is the end of our association with the two famous British surveyors. Soon after their meeting with the troublesome Minuets, the entire survey party set the great stone in the corner of the state of Maryland and moved their camp westward. Finally, from Dixon's point of view, serious attention was directed toward the Mason-Dixon line that divides Maryland and Pennsylvania and the other section that divides Maryland and Delaware.

The entire party followed the paths opened by the sweat and brawn of the ax-men, and their contributions live on to this day. Even at the approach of the 21st century, the Mason-Dixon Line is known throughout the world as an engineering marvel and the informal dividing line between the North and South.

But, for the rest of his natural life, until he died in the City of Philadelphia, Charles Mason told those he met of how a strange, fat child of a Maryland fishwoman, had eaten his greatest invention. He also explained how in less than a minute's time, the hungry little demon had consumed thousands of pounds sterling, in one single bite. Mason also was annoyed when he discovered that London officials had awarded the prize for the chronometer's invention while he was in the New World, working on the Mason-Dixon Line— about the same time his invention was swallowed.

As years passed, the Minuit family moved to Pennsylvania, living in Chadds Ford, Marcus Hook and nearby Chester. Eventually, Fithian Minuit, who grew up to be recognized by his rotund figure, became known throughout the region as one of the most agreeable, industrious and honest peddlers in the colonies.

He eventually took an interest in carpentry, clock making and repair and opened a shop in the small village of Christiana, Delaware, in a modest stone and frame home beside the narrow bridge that spanned the small creek.

In his shop was a vast array of clocks, sundials, watches and hour-burning candles. He would travel the Delaware Valley and Chesapeake Bay region, buying from individuals with homes along the Smyrna, Bohemia, Sassafras and Chester rivers. He was well known from the St. Jones River in Dover to the Brandywine River in Wilmington, and his shop offered excellent grandfather clocks and smaller pieces that he would repair, trade and sell.

74

It was said he had "the gift" with time pieces. Beside the door on the inside of Fithian's shop, which was full of the sound of ticking, was a sign listing his many services. Across the wall, behind his desk, was a large plaque inscribed with the words: "Time never stops, even though the timepiece does."

Each person who made contact with the timekeeper found him most agreeable. But it seemed strange that such a friendly chap could not find a wifely companion.

That, however, changed when Fithian met Martha, the daughter of a sea captain from Port Penn, Delaware, who had come to the Christiana shop seeking Fithian's services for a ship chronometer.

A friendship grew between the two men and, whenever the captain returned from his voyage, Fithian was invited to the captain's home. On his last trip, knowing the fondness that was growing between his daughter and the clockmaker, the captain asked Fithian to care for Martha in the event the captain never returned from sea. Slightly embarrassed but flattered and delighted, Fithian agreed.

Within a year, the captain's ship was lost in a storm at sea, and the clockmaker fulfilled his bargain to his friend. Martha and Fithian were married, and for both it was a joyous occasion for it was obvious that they were truly in love.

On their wedding night, the wife was startled at the steady rhythmic sound coming from her husband's side of the bed.

Fearing first an illness, then some sort of superstition or witchcraft, she eased out of the bed. Carefully, Martha searched the entire bedroom for the source of the steady rhythmic beat. After looking on the bureau, on the night stands, under the bed and in the closet, she found no reasonable source of the strange rhythmic sound.

Fithian, observing her concern, pulled her to his side. The sound intensified as she rested her head upon his chest. Slowly, he explained the story of his unusual meeting at a very young age with Charles Mason. At least he explained it as it had been told to him by his mother and others in his family.

Together they laughed and decided that the sound of Mason's invention would represent their mutual love, and it would beat until the end of all time, even past their death here on Earth.

For more than 40 years the couple lived together, until Martha died. She was buried in the New London "Hardshell" Baptist graveyard, off South Bank Road.

Fithian devoted himself to his work even more after her departure, and he took comfort in playing his favorite fiddle. After a long day's work, he would sit in his rocker on the front porch of his shop, swaying back and forth as if keeping time to a secret rhythm. Some neighbors passing by said he often seemed to be talking to someone, although the area was vacant of anyone else nearby.

To visitors to his shop he would suggest strongly that time not be used foolishly. "Be sure to use time wisely," Fithian warned, "for the second hand never stops its movement around the dial, and the minute and hour hands chase right behind. And, for sure, the days, months and years follow at a steady rate. Time, which seems so brief and slight when measured in lone seconds and single minutes, adds up all to quickly. And time, like life itself, passes on rapidly and is lost to us all forever."

One weekend, a passing wagon with a group of hunters out seeking game discovered Fithian in the graveyard, by the side of the spot where his wife, Martha, was buried. At the age of close to 80, he had fallen into a state of deep eternal sleep. Those who found him said his face seemed fixed in a smile, for he was finally reunited with his beloved Martha.

Out of respect, drivers of passing coaches and families in farm wagons stopped. As word of his death spread, both city dwellers and country people came to pay their respects to the pleasant, well-known clockmaker who had given the best of times to them all.

They laid him to rest beside his bride, and there he remains, for all eternity.

And even today, hundreds of years after his death, the legend, the story, the folktale of Fithian Minuet and his noteworthy meeting with Charles Mason still lives on.

While his ancient gravestone is cracked and worn, and the hand-carved writing is faded and gone, and the ground within the cemetery walls is sloped and sagging . . . if the wind isn't blowing too hard, and if the waters of the White Clay Creek aren't too swift . . . and if there are no passing cars racing on the nearby narrow road . . . and—most importantly—if you know which stone to approach, then take a moment and kneel on the damp grass, as so many have done before, gently place your ear against the cold, stone grave marker and wait, be patient and listen.

If it's meant to be, and if you truly believe in the legend, you might hear the steady "tick—tick—tick"—of the Ticking Tomb.

And those who have heard it smile with satisfaction, for they say they believe Fithian Minuit is there, telling us that Charles Mason's chronometer, still held tightly by the pleasant colonial clockmaker, remains in safe keeping, and in good operating order, for all eternity.

Author's note: The Hardshell Baptist Church and Graveyard still exist. The site serves as a visitor's center for the State of Pennsylvania portion of the White Clay Creek Preserve. A sign on the side of the building identifies the site as the "London Tract Meeting House."

The easiest way to locate the Ticking Tomb is to ask the park guide or a representative in the converted church. However, if no one is on duty, enter the graveyard through the white, wooden gate and head toward the doors of the church/meeting house/park center. Walk to the end of the sidewalk and then continue in the direction of 11 o'clock on Charles Mason's timepiece.

Approximately 20 feet past the end of the building, next to the small, elevated, heart-shaped gravestone of "John Devonold," you will find the Ticking Tomb. The gray stone maker is flush with the ground and bears the initials "R.S." or "R.C." (Why R.S. or R.C. if the grave is that of Fithian Minuit? I do not know and cannot guess.)

This is said to be the Ticking Tomb. Park representatives also may point out an elevated, brick, rectangular gravesite that also has been referred to as the Ticking Tomb. Keep in mind, over hundreds of years legends are changed and different versions passed on.

A note of caution, do not think that the Ticking Tomb is "outside" the gates of the cemetery in the midst of a small, grassy island, at the intersection of adjoining roads. This stone structure that looks like a set of steps that have lost its house is exactly that—steps used as a carriage mount for ladies, so they would not have difficulty entering carriages or stagecoaches. I've been told that some people have knelt and placed their ears to the top platform of the carriage mount, thinking the set of steps is the Ticking Tomb.

Save yourself unnecessary embarrassment and spend your time more fruitfully, searching the interior of the graveyard or asking directions from park personnel.

Don't Sleep On the Beach

Officials and residents of beach towns and seaside resorts go out of their way to minimize bad news, especially when it happens between Memorial Day weekend and Labor Day.

Tourist season, you know.

Wild parties, traffic accidents, rental disputes and parking problems are kept as quiet as possible and, definitely, never appear in the front pages of the local newspapers. The unwritten, unspoken, unbroken—but totally understood—rule, observed by image conscious merchants and town managers alike is: Nothing bad happens during tourist season.

But, in the late 1960s—at a small but popular, Southern New Jersey beach town—something horrible did happen. The details have been kept secret, but several of those who are aware of the incident believe the bizarre and deadly tragedy has happened more than once.

A group of four young boys, all between the ages of 10 and 12, were spending their fourth summer together. They looked forward to meeting each year at the Shore and spending the hot days swimming, fishing, exploring the sand dunes and, in particular, digging for pirate treasure.

During an overnight campout on the beach, on the edge of an abandoned military base, Ace, the largest of the four boys, waited until his friends were sound asleep. At 3:30 in the morning, with the steady sound of the nearby waves in the background as cover, the 12-year-old prankster silently slid out of his sleeping bag and headed for a pre-selected position in the darkness, just on the other side the dunes.

Quietly, he dug into the sand and pulled out a dark plastic bag. He had hidden it at the site the day before. Ace smiled, eager to get into the costume, approach the campfire, let out a scream and scare his friends half to death.

As quietly as possible, he pulled out the dark baggy pants and heavy black boots. The long dark blue coat was next. He noticed how its gold buttons reflected the light of the full moon. The fake beard, earring and eyepatch would add a bit of authenticity, he thought, laughing to himself. Lastly, he dug deeper into the cool, crusty sand and pulled out the sword. Its blade was dull, but the weapon was real metal, not a plastic, dime store imitation.

After he was dressed, Ace stood on the ridge of the sandy hill and looked out to sea. This is the same scene the real pirates must have looked at hundreds of years ago, he thought. Ace imagined how the ancient seamen felt, how the buccaneers talked and what evil deeds they would perform if they came upon a campfire like the one warming his sleeping companions.

Slowly, Ace stepped, heading toward the fading embers. Only 30 feet to go.

He was so excited. He planned to move into the center of the campsite, scream at the top of his lungs and wave the sword in circles just inches above the heads of his friends.

The first thing they'll see when they open their eyes is Blackbeard the Pirate, ready to chop off their heads, Ace thought. He could hardly hold back his laughter as he imagined his friends' horrified reactions.

Less than 20 feet to go.

His pace was slow as he watched the sand, avoiding shells, twigs, paper and any other debris that would make noise and alert the slumbering campers.

What was left of the fire's glow was reflected on his face. The sword was getting heavy, so he dragged it behind, its point leaving a thin, shallow trail in the beach sand.

He was 10 feet from the center of the camp. The warmth of the fire touched his face.

No one had stirred. He was close enough to hear the steady breathing of the sleepers.

The most difficult moment of the surprise attack had arrived. Carefully, Ace selected his steps, placing his feet slowly and silently . . . navigating his body through the multicolored sleeping bags. Now, finally, he was in the midst of the open-air lair, and all of his victims were unaware that they were only seconds away from a fright night to remember.

With the moon providing an eerie illumination, and it's reflection glowing off the ocean, Ace looked out and smiled. But, within seconds a sick look of fear froze every muscle on his face. He did not, could not, scream at his friends. He was unable to startle them out of their sound sleep. Instead, the sword he had raised, the one with the dull blade, was frozen in mid air.

Silent, stiff and scared, he saw forms that were walking, apparently gliding, out of the sea. They came from the inside of the white surf and round, inky blackness of the rolling waves. There were two . . . five . . . eight . . . 12—a dozen full-sized men.

Holding the sword above his head like a statue, Ace's mind told him that the figures were not men. NO!, he realized, THEY'RE PIRATES!

But, as if in a dream, he could not move. Try as he did, not one muscle, finger or limb responded to his efforts to scream or run. But the strangely dressed phantoms, who looked solid and real and human, floated silently about him. With ease, they passed by, around and through Ace as if he wasn't there.

The unearthly visitors were talking to each other, but Ace could not hear a word. He just watched in a horrified state of silence, waiting for them to notice him and terrified of what would happen when they did.

The tall man with the three-cornered hat and long beard was giving orders, first pointing, then apparently shouting and waving his arms at the others. Ace decided the leader was telling the others to speed up the pace, to move about more quickly.

On that dark night, in a rented costume, with fake whiskers and a plastic eyepatch, Ace watched on a deserted beach as the spirits of those long dead picked up his three young summer beach friends and carried them away forever . . . into the cold black ocean.

After the shore party disappeared, all that remained were empty sleeping bags, sand-coated canteens and crushed snack wrappers scattered around a cold, dead fire.

His friends were kidnapped in the arms of strangers, wearing clothes from another time, ghosts from a different dimension and place, far away from pizza dinners, video arcades and boardwalk caramel popcorn.

Edwin disappeared first.

Georgie was second.

And Little Mikey was the last to be swallowed up by the strangers and the sea.

When he could finally move again, Ace wished it all had been an intense, horrifying nightmare, but the empty sleeping bags and the bloodstains on his metal sword confirmed that something real had occurred.

Ace ran from bag to bag, searching, looking, praying and calling out their names—"MIKEY! GEORGIEEEE! EDWINNNNN!"

But the shoreline was empty, the sun just starting to climb out of the thin strip that divides the surface of the vast sea and the beginning of the endless sky.

Ace was still in the costume. He was worried, and his sword with all the blood bothered him.

Had they mistaken me for a pirate? he wondered. Is that why I was spared?

He was only 12, but he wasn't stupid. He had to get help, and he had to tell someone about what happened before they blamed him.

Leaving the weapon and heavy pirate coat behind, he ran toward town, stopping the first person he met—an early morning walker enjoying the start of a quiet day at the beach. Shaking, Ace shouted the highlights of his bizarre tale in bits and snippets. The police were called. State park investigators arrived soon afterwards.

They found the bloody sword with no problem. It was resting beside Ace's bedroll. But they also discovered that the insides of each of the other three sleeping bags were soaked with fresh blood.

The lifeguard boat with hired divers continued searching through the late afternoon. The three bodies were never found.

What bothered the police most of all was the lack of footprints, or any indication of a struggle or that the three boys had been dragged off by anyone or anything.

"It was like they were beamed up into thin air," one officer said.

"Shark bait for sure," others whispered.

Ace told and retold his story—about a band of pirates coming out of the water and carting away his friends.

The police and his parents believe he's crazy.

The doctors and expert psychiatrists (he's been to many) believe he has "problems accepting reality and needs years of analysis to bring him back to an acceptable level to exist in mainstream society." They don't think he killed his friends, but they don't believe his story either.

To tell the truth, no one wants to believe what Ace still swears that he saw on the beach that night.

Eventually, the police gave up and moved on to other, more solvable crimes. The reports of the incident are buried in the deepest corner of the department's incident files. No bad news during tourist season, you know. The officers involved were told not to discuss the case, and the parents of the missing boys don't go back to vacation at that Jersey Shore beach town any longer.

But cops talk . . . while at conventions, at family parties, in bars and during off duty hours . . . and people are more than eager to listen.

If you hang out at this popular resort town—located on the Atlantic Coast north of Cape May and south of Atlantic City—be sure to keep your ears open. It's amazing what you might hear. But if you walk down on the beach at night, don't go alone. Never go alone.

If you're unlucky, you just might see two . . . five . . . eight . . . 12—a dozen full-sized men—come out of the water, walk up onto the beach and leave no footprints. If that occurs, just remember what happened to Georgie, Edwin and Little Mikey—and don't let it happen to you.

Author's note: Pirates, including such famous personalities as Blackbeard and Captain Kidd, did frequent the New Jersey and Delaware coasts in the 17th and 18th centuries. Many believe these buccaneers left behind chests filled with treasure, and that they return, with members of their crews, to locate and guard them.

Each year, dozens of young children and adults disappear while on vacation at beaches throughout the country. Many are believed to have drowned, become lost in the tidal marshes or run off on their own. But, several cases remain unsolved, unexplained and—to many who learn the truth—unbelievable.

Chat With a Bat

Ron Powers slammed down the phone and was beginning to go off the deep end. His editor, Harvey Blake, had given Ron a last-minute assignment—a full-length feature. Still fuming from the latest of a long series of confrontations, Ron threw his cigar onto his desk and pulled his 260-pound frame out of his worn swivel chair. Breathing heavily, he headed for the editor's office to protest in person.

Blake said he wanted a story on the American Adventure Arcade, a two-bit, second-rate, fleabag carnival that came through town every summer. It had already been in the cornfield on the edge of town for six nights, and this evening was its last night before the menagerie of misfits pulled up stakes and moved to another one-horse town on the peninsula.

All of the sudden, everything was in a major crisis, mainly because the stupid intern who had been assigned the story had been involved in a traffic accident in Baltimore. Ron Powers, who had been with the paper for 12 years and usually had his pick of assignments, was given the intern's job.

Bursting into Blake's office, Ron pounded the desk and went through a litany of reasons why he shouldn't give up his evening. He was a professional and had faithfully served the *Chronicle Gazette* for a dozen years. His beat was hard news. He admitted that an investigative feature was fine, even enjoyable once or twice a year, but this Mickey Mouse assignment was beneath someone of his professional stature. Plus, he had promised Stella, his steady squeeze for the last 10 years, a quiet dinner for two at the best restaurant in town.

Blake nodded. He even smiled.

Ron thought he had made his point and was on the winning end of the argument. Then his editor recited his "needs of the publication" speech and mentioned that Ron had stood up poor Stella more times than he could count. The frustrated reporter knew he had gone down for the count.

The editor's final words were an insult. "Get out there, Ron. The change will do you good. Mingle with the stars. Get the smell of the fresh country air into your lungs. Bring me back a feature that I'll want to find space for on page one. Show me your stuff. Give me something off the wall, something abnormal and news-worthy, the hidden, exotic, overlooked pearl that only a man with your expertise can discover."

Ron turned without a word and let the slamming door serve as his reply.

Five hours later, still annoyed and insulted, the angry reporter strolled the converted cornfield. The smell of roasting peanuts, hot popcorn, dried elephant dung and sweet cotton candy mingled in the fall evening breeze.

At that moment, the aggravated reporter found everything abnormal. Midgets, misfits and weirdos of various shapes and colors were parading down the midway. But, he thought, at least they're happy. They seemed to be doing what they wanted and, probably, the traveling carnival was the nearest thing to a family that any of the poor souls would ever find.

When Ron was a kid, the make-believe world of the visiting fireman's carnival with its frightening characters and neon-lit rides seemed exciting, glamorous and scary. Looking more critically, now the stars were older, fatter and balder. The glitter was held together with mended costumes, and wrinkles were hidden beneath heavy make-up.

The reporter decided to give the midway a second pass and, hopefully, locate Blake's abnormal feature. Then, a sign, leaning beside the tent next to the Ferris wheel, caught his eye:

VAMPIRE
Only One in Captivity
Baron Anton Zantanski
(from the Old Country)
Two shows nightly
NO MATINEES

Chuckling, Ron paid the toothless woman in the cramped ticket booth $4. A grizzled Mickey Rooney look-alike stood near the tent flap collecting stubs. Ron decided to pump the barker, who was tapping the tip of a cheap toy cane against the tip of a bright green derby.

"Is this for real, Pop?" joked Ron.

"As I live and breath, Sonny," the old man replied, spitting out a chaw of tobacco coated with sweet ginger brandy.

"Come on, Pop, I'm no school kid. You can level with me."

"I is, Son," Mickey said. "This fella's the best. I tell ya, if this here Baron ain't fer real, he's sure the closest thing to it."

"What about the vampire bit?"

"Well," whispered the short man as he took the reporter's arm to pull him aside, "I ain't never seed the guy durin' the daytime. Not never!"

"That's probably because you're sleeping off a drunk most of the time," Ron said, laughing at the cleverness of his insult.

"No! NO!" the old man said, raising his hand as if he were swearing in court. Suddenly, becoming more serious and talking even more softly, he continued, "I's tellin' ya the truth. This guy, he gives me the heebie jeebies. Look, he owns this here whole show, and he don't never talk to nobody. Never! Does all his message sendin' through that big goon over there." The barker pointed toward "Otto the Great," a 7-foot giant lifting barbells outside on a stage two tents away.

"Come on, Pop. Cut with the fairy tales. That cheap booze is frying what's left of your brain." Ron laughed as he pulled away from the old man.

"To hell with you, Sonny! I ain't 'bout to stand here and waste my breath if you're gonna give me a loada crap back. 'Sides, my line's backin' up," the barker snapped. "So if you're gonna go in, go in, or hit the damn road you come in on."

"Okay. Okay," Ron said, laughing. "You're really pretty good, you know that, Pop? You should try out for the movies with that act of yours."

Ron was still smiling as he entered the tent and took a seat on a worn and scratched wooden bench in the center of the tent. It was the last show—11 o'clock—and the crowd wasn't that large, less than 20 people in a seating area that could accommodate about 50.

Most of the customers were teenagers who would use the screams and darkness as an opportunity to make out before they had to head for home.

Without warning, the lights dropped and the tent became a black world of total darkness.

"G-O-O-O-O-D . . . E-E-E-VENING!" spoke a slow, heavily-accented voice. "Velcome to my traveling castle."

A few of the young girls screamed. Their dates shook their heads and laughed.

Gradually, a soft, red glow filled the tent, eventually allowing the audience to distinguish the form of a figure moving toward the center of the low stage. A chalk-faced vampire, dressed in a black tuxedo and red-lined cape gazed upon the attentive audience.

During the next 40 minutes, screams of fright and outbursts of laughter indicated the audience's approval of what Ron considered a surprisingly well-done performance. The special effects included disappearances, coffins, sizzling skin, flying bats, sharp fangs, and, the usual finale—a wooden stake through the vampire's heart.

As he exited the tent, the reporter smiled. He had found his story—an interview with the baron.

The midget barker was totally wasted and lying behind the tent on a small bed of straw. Annoyed at being awakened by Ron the Unbeliever, the carnival employee eventually was able to focus his thoughts and gave directions to the Baron's office. And, for good measure, the drunk also told Ron where he could go.

Ron located the large black trailer, parked on the edge of the grounds and backing up to an empty field. He knocked twice, but there was no answer.

He rapped a third time. When no one responded, he tried the silver aluminum doorknob.

It was unlocked.

As he pushed gently on the door, he was startled by an accented voice that came from the dark interior.

"That is not a very proper ting for you to do."

Looking into the dimly lit room, Ron recognized the Baron's smiling, make-up coated face.

Nervously, the reporter tried to explain, "I'm with the local newspaper . . . . Looking for a story. Mister? Mister?"

"BARON Zantanski," the star replied. His voice had the thick Slavic accent and measured theatrical tone he had used on stage.

"Right! Baron. That's what I meant," Ron said, regaining his composure. "I wanted to meet you," he explained, "want to interview you about your act. I was quite impressed, and I think you would make a great story."

"Ah, my tanks to you, dear sir," the Baron replied, gesturing that Ron enter into the aluminum box. "It is so nice to be appreciated by someone of educated substance. Yes. I vill be so kind enough to grant to you an audience. Now, please feel free to enter into my chamber vith me. Ve vill sit and share some varm vine during our little chat together."

Ron walked further into the trailer, heading for the low red light in the far corner of the room.

As his eyes adjusted to the minimal level of illumination, Ron's expression revealed his astonishment.

"You seem to like vhat you see."

"This is magnificent," the visitor replied.

"Ah, so it is. You vill please to be seated here, and I vill be but only a brief moment. For I must dispose of these theatrical garments and dress in attire more appropriate for entertaining such a distinguished member of the press."

With the Baron gone, Ron got up and explored the room, impressed with the ornate furnishings, thick paneling and expensive paintings. If they were real, or even good reproductions, thought the reporter, the contents of the trailer were worth a fortune. This guy must be loaded.

Sporting a black and gold smoking jacket and holding two glasses of dark red wine, the Baron returned. "I do hope you vill find this most agreeable, Mister?"

"Powers. *Chronicle Gazette*. Thanks. I could use a drink." Ron nodded as he accepted the wine.

"To your eternal life, Mister Powers Chronicle Gazette," toasted the Baron.

"Likewise," Ron said, raising his glass and downing the liquid. "It's tasty. A bit warm," he said, somewhat surprised.

"Ah, yes. I do so love my fine vines to be varm or hot. Never chilled or cold." Grinning, the Baron added, "I find them to taste best at body temperature. So? Vhat is the nature of vhat you vant to talk vith me of?"

Ron, erect on a stiff, ornately carved, throne-like seat, explained the assignment his editor had given him earlier in the day.

The Baron listened intently, then asked, "So, this editor, he is unavare of the focus you have decided to select, and is likevise ignorant of your exact vhereabouts?"

"Well, strictly speaking, he has no idea what I will write about. I'm supposed to turn the story in by late tomorrow night. When I saw your show, I knew it—I mean, you—were the one. And when I heard you owned the carnival, well, that just added . . . . "

Abruptly rising, the Baron snapped, "And from vhat source did you determine such a thing?"

"Some old man. The barker outside your tent. Why, is there a problem?"

"I do not desire for such details to be of public knowledge. I so do treasure my privacy."

Ron smiled. "I can understand that. No problem. I won't include it in the piece. It's not important to the focus of our story. Okay?"

"My sincere thanks," said the Baron, as he smiled and returned to his black leather seat.

"By the way," asked Ron, "could you turn on a brighter light? That red glow is making it hard for me to take notes."

"Ah, but I am so sorry. It is from my physician's orders. My eyes," the Baron said, pointing a long, bony finger toward his black pupils. "The brightness of the white lights, it causes them such frightful pain. You will please to be able to bear such an inconvenience for my sake?"

"Oh, sure," said Ron, running a finger around his open collar. "Then, maybe you could just open a window."

The Baron shook his head weakly, "But, alas, I am again so very pained, for I have not any vindows. Security reasons, as you can vell understand. But, allow me, please, to bring you another goblet of sveet varm vine. I am so sure that it vill improve your troubled spirits."

By the time the Baron returned, Ron was pressing his shirt-sleeve against his forehead, trying to remove the growing mist of perspiration.

"Here ve are my young friend," the Baron said as he passed the crystal glass to the reporter. "And see, I have even placed in it a piece of cold ice, especially for your very sake."

"Thanks. That should help."

"Vell, vhat now shall ve discuss?"

Ron looked across the room and the Baron seemed to actually fade into the dark overstuffed chair.

"How about your act? How did you come up with the idea?"

"Ah, I must say to you that it was but a natural selection. My parents, they vere famous performers, in the great Polish circus in the Old World. They traveled all throughout Europe, the Middle East, and, from my date of birth, I vas vith them. At a very early age, I assisted in their productions."

"I see, a family theatrical background. Good connection. What kind of act did they have?" asked Ron, noticing that his writing seemed a bit slower than usual.

"Ah, but they, too, were also vampyrs," replied the Baron, smiling and tapping the long, sharp points of his manicured nails.

The reporter chuckled softly. "You mean to say that their act was also a vampire act?"

"No," countered the Baron calmly, "I do mean to say to you: Yes! Their act was a vampyr production. And, yes again, they vere, the two of them, both also vampyrs."

"Okay, fine," Ron said, waving his left hand and signaling he was not going to get hung up on a minor point, risk antagonizing his subject and ruin the entire story.

"Ah, you see, but you do not believe even vhat you do presently see. Vhat then do you believe me to be, Mister Powers Chronicle Gazette?"

"A clever magician and," Ron pointed to the room's antiques and paintings, "a very successful businessman. Call me Ron."

"You do so flatter me, kind sir. So this does but truly appear to be such the case. But, I tell you in the strictest confidence and vith pride—because you appear to be the type of intelligent person one is able to trust—I, too, am also very much a genuine vampyr."

The reporter shifted uneasily in his chair. This bozo, thought Ron, isn't working with a full deck.

Ron decided to humor the counterfeit Baron. Besides, two could play this kind of game. The reporter decided to complete the interview and then show the nitwit with the fake Count

Spirits Between the Bays

Dracula accent and comic book make-up how a real investigative
reporter operates. And, what a great story it will be, he thought, trying to suppress his smile. This would be one of his best, an interview with a nut that really believed he was the Prince of Darkness.
Blake was going to get his abnormal feature and then some.

"If it's true, that you are an actual vampire," Ron said, "you
must have had some difficult times. Not being able to walk
around during the day, few social opportunities, a limited diet,
things like that."

"Vell, it is trying for some of my associates," replied the
Baron, totally serious. "But, I am most truly and basically a night
type of being. Therefore, I do not at all mind the lateness of the
hours. Besides, I do not follow the theater, the opera. I relish solitary valks along the river, especially during the fullness of the
moon. So, I accept, and in all honesty, I do so enjoy my lot."

"How long have you been a vampire?"

"Since forever!" the Baron exclaimed. Flashing a larger smile,
he added, "My young new friend, you must understand that I,
Baron Zantanski, am a thoroughbred vampyr, having been born of
two undead parents. This is so very important that you must be
sure to mark down and report it vith true accuracy," he said, pointing to Ron's notebook.

"No other undead has ever pierced my pure throat. I vas not, I
repeat, I vas never first a humanlike creature who vas made a
vampire by such a crass and traumatic penetrations. Again, I say
this to you, it is a most important distinction among the legion of
the undead. And, I demand that this be so printed in your essay. I
have, I do hope, made my desires expressedly clear?"

"Yes, quite clear," Ron said. "I'll get it all in there. So let me
ask you the question in another way, What year were you born?"

The Baron, now more calm and relaxed, replied with ease. "In
the year 1132. So, I am, by your style of annual birthdate calcula-
tions, at this present time, 867 years in being. But, who my age
concerns himself with time? Vhen one can live on forever, vhat
means a few hundred of years?"

"But, you look so good, so fresh, so youthful."

"Ah, friend Ron, you are too kind. My sincerest thanks to you,
kind sir. It is most surely due to my special diet—only varm fluids,
never solids. Long flights in the evenings, such aerobic exercise
helps me to maintain my most youthful appearance."

90

"What about your childhood? Was it a happy one?"

"But, yes!" The Baron seemed especially pleased with the question, probably because it gave him an opportunity to remember pleasant experiences during his youth.

"It vas vonderful. My friends and I, ve vould romp in the voods below the castle. All the night long, ve frolicked vith our pet volves. And, of course, often vithout permission, ve vould sneak into the village and terrorize the stupid peasants. Ha! Those vere the days!"

"What about your parents? Didn't they care for you?"

"Vell, as you can, I'm so certainly very sure imagine, so vell, raising a growing family vas very difficult. My father, and even in some cases and instances, my mother, vould have to go to vork all the night through. And ve had great difficulty securing the services of baby sitters. So, ve vere often left to our own pleasures and delights.

"I recall how ve vould play the game Hide and Zeek, and sing little coffin songs like, 'Bite the farmer on his throat, next his vife and last his goat.'

"But, I vill tell you this now. The game I did hate the most vas Spotlight. I can still feel the pain vhen the light from the blazing lantern shown so harshly on my cute little red eyes."

Ron was running out of questions, but it was too good an experience to stop. "Didn't you have any chores, any work to do around the castle?"

"But, of course. Ve had to keep the castle spotless clean, in case that ve vould have visitors fly in from the South of America or Africa. And, if very good, my father vould take us on a night visit to the village, scaring the peasants as they ran around vith garlic necklaces and crosses on their chests.

"I recall still how my mother and I vould hold open the little sack as father brought out to us a juicy baby or a plump ripe virgin. Mother and I vould drag the screaming creature to the cellar and drain it and prepare a nice hot red stew for vhen father returned from a hard night looting the countryside."

"You seem to have a strong affection for your father. Is he still . . . alive?"

"Please, he is not," the Baron said, dropping his head on his chest. "A bearded lunatic, named Von Helsing—who vent on safari chasing vampyrs for sport—murdered my noble parent in Tibet.

He vas the same insane professor that vas made famous by the English author Stoker. But, please, it is so very painful to my veak heart. I vould rather not to discuss it vith you."

"Of course. Let's talk about something else. Did you go to school?"

The Baron was obviously offended. "My young friend," he snapped, "Do you believe that ve are uncultured barbarians? Vhy of course ve had studies! Ve had to be seated in our dungeon classroom on many nights, promptly at sunset and for two hours. Ve studied the subjects of theater, music, art, science—all the finer things of the afterlife. Ah, and the languages—my favorites—the Latin, the Greek, the Chinese. The list, it can go on and on."

"This is all very interesting," Ron said. With hesitation, he approached a delicate subject, asking, "Are there many vampires around today. I get the impression that they're a dying breed. Frankly, you're the first one I've ever encountered."

"Vell, Mister Ron, I vill say this to you now at this time, there are many more of us among you than you vould, of course, be so pleased to admit. Vhy, vhen we have our reunions, ve must rent the most spacious of facilities to accommodate our large num-bers. You may even find this of some interest, some of our oldest associates do reside in your immediate area, and they do conduct your normal types of business. For amusement, they pass the time as toll collectors, night watchmen, janitors, police and fire personnel. As you are most probably able to imagine, professions of doctors and nurses are very popular vith the vampyrs.

"But, the most favorite of positions, having the highest pres-tige among the family of the undead, is the undertaker. This most sought after occupation provides so many of us with an unlimited supply of the source of eternal life. In the true spirit of free enter-prise, they sell their excess varm vine to friends and associates."

"Sounds great, a real American success story," Ron observed.

"Ah, but it most truly is," the Baron said. "There is, however, only one problem—greed. As an educated consumer, you must be careful and learn of those to trust and those to avoid. Many in this field attempt to make for themselves a quick killing by vater-ing down the product. I vill say this, from actual experience, it is so very annoying vhen you, in good faith, pay to a person the full price for a quality type of product and then do receive instead sec-ond-class merchandise. But, ve know how to deal vith them."

"How's that?"

"Those who have complaints join to administer vigilante justice by paying the offender a midnight visit. Our little group vill fill the thief's mouth with garlic, disconnect the head and drive an oaken stake through the heart."

"You guys don't fool around."

"Please, Mister Ron, people or persons, but not guys. Ve are not in any form or shape a sexist group."

"I'm sorry. It was just an expression."

"I do accept your most kind apologies."

"Do you find it difficult, at times, being a vampire?"

The Baron laughed. "Like all circumstances, it does at certain times have its trying moments. For of instance, did you ever attempt to get dressed and combed to attend an important function, but are unable to view your own appearance.

"Ve do not cast a reflection in the mirror glass. Fortunately, for my case, I have my charming vife, the Baroness, to check my hair, my bow tie, my flesh-colored make-up. And I must do so similarly for her.

"Vhy, I precisely do recall one chilly October evening. I made an appearance at the annual gala of my favorite charity, the Blood Bank. As my sweetest Baroness was unable to review my appearance prior to my most hasty departure, I vas never so humiliated in all of my several lives.

"My hair vas not properly coiffured; my cosmetics vere smeared; and even my cravat vas crooked. With luck, a goodly number of my colleagues of the night vere also present. They did assist me to adjust my appearance accordingly."

"Sounds like a rough night on the town."

"But so it vas! You can vell imagine that I have never been able to enjoy the certain simple treasures of your human life. The afternoon picnics or the days on the sandymost beaches. And, only on one or two very threatening occasions did I ever glimpse the most earliest rays of the sunrise. But, you can vell imagine the chance I did risk to do so. Now, I confine my viewing of the morning sun to my video machine, but it is still painful and I must wear dark glasses.

"So, as the saying goes, 'Ve all of us each do have our little crosses to bear.' " Following the quip, the Baron let out a healthy laugh.

"Your accommodations are very well decorated," Ron said, rubbing his eyes to stay awake.

"Ah, yes, it is so. These are but temporary quarters, my home away from home, if you vill. My many castles are superbly gorgeous. I vill take you there vith me one day. You vould like, yes?"

Thinking no, Ron said, "Yes."

Rising, the Baron moved to the center of the parlor, stopping beneath a glowing red chandelier, "Please, come vith me and I vill escort you throughout my modest traveling abode."

Ron rose unsteadily, almost falling. Gathering his balance, he focused on his host and followed the Baron down an ill-lit corridor. Each room they passed was decorated to correspond to a different historical period.

Opening the door at the end of the long hall, the Baron said, "I offer this chamber to my many guests." Ron noticed the bedroom had a private bath and more antiques than a fine estate.

"Over here is the kitchen, the formal dining room and this is my private study. Ah, and here, please to come this vay to view my master bed chamber. I do believe that the Baroness is at home this night. She vould simply experience a stake attack in her heart if she did not also meet vith you."

The Baron turned the gold handle and pushed open the heavy brown door. Inside, a soft glow, identical to the lamps in the rest of the trailer, washed the walls in a pink haze. Ron rubbed his eyes, trying to follow his host as the Baron seemed to glide to the distant end of the room.

As Ron's feet sank into the wine-colored carpeting, he bumped into a large coffee table resting in the center of floor. The reporter noticed his reflection in the highly polished glass. The Baron stood, grinning, a few feet away, beside what appeared to be a huge glass wall.

"I vould like to introduce to you my vife, the Baroness Zantanska!"

Suddenly and silently, the mirrored panels began to move, revealing a secret room and inside was a flat box. As Ron moved closer, toward the rectangular container, the lid began to rise. Within moments, he was beside the Baron and looking down on a beautiful dark-haired woman who was resting in what appeared to be a plush, double-bedded coffin.

Ron thought his heart had stopped and nearly fell to the floor, but the Baron grabbed the reporter by the shoulders. Gaining the use of his legs, he stared into the magnificent box, but his head still had that uncomfortable, light feeling that you get just before you are about to pass out.

Again, his legs started to melt, like two thin icicles in the afternoon sun. But, the Baron shook the reporter and pointed into the coffin.

The Baroness was a stunning, shapely seductive creature. Ron's eyes locked on her bright red lips. The black lace of her gown contrasted with the pale pink ruffles that formed a fringe around the satin tomb.

Abruptly, her eyes opened and captured those of her onlooker. Ron tried to turn away, but his head, his whole body was frozen, unable to move. His feet left the floor. He felt his entire body being lifted, carried.

He was staring at the ceiling, but he didn't care, couldn't do anything about if he had tried.

In his last moments of consciousness, he recognized the craggy, marred face of Otto the Great. The muscular giant held Ron's body like a baby controlling a small toy. Slowly the Baron's subject lowered the reporter into the bed of soft satin.

"No! Stop!" the victim pleaded, but his voice was no more than a brief whisper. The only beings that heard his useless effort were both salivating and baring their gleaming, canine teeth.

Ron closed his eyes, hoping that the bad dream would end. He could smell the stale breath coming from both sides of his neck and the hissing sounds of animal-like anticipation entering both his ears.

He felt the soft female-like body pressed against his left side. Stronger muscles, belonging to the creature in the tuxedo, leaned against the right portion of his chest.

As the breathing became louder, more passionate, Ron noticed the stench of dried blood and wet mold of the vampire's home earth that was seeping from its hiding place beneath the pink satin covering on the base of the coffin.

Ron opened his eyes one final time and saw the giant's massive outline against the glow of the Baron's bed chamber. Then, the reluctant reporter, who was searching for the ultimate abnormal story, heard the lid of the coffin click shut. The rosy world turned to ink black.

His two hosts pressed down against his chest and began to fight over their favorite sections of his anatomy. Clawing and hissing, the Baron and Baroness tore into Ron's body like a pair of hungry dogs fighting over a single bowl of food.

His final scream reached no farther then the soft satin lid of the coffin that pressed against the dying reporter's forehead.

As Otto the Great locked his master's bedroom door, he heard soft coos and gurgling's of delight, and he knew the loving couple would enjoy the rest of their evening.

About the Author

E d Okonowicz, a Delaware native and freelance writer,
is an editor and writer at the University of Delaware,
where he earned a bachelor's degree in music education
and a master's degree in communication.

Also a professional storyteller, Ed is a member of the National
Storytelling Association. He presents programs at country inns,
retirement homes, schools, libraries, private gatherings, public
events, Elderhostels and theaters in the Mid-Atlantic region.

He specializes in local legends and folklore of the Delaware
and Chesapeake Bays, as well as topics related to the Eastern Shore
of Maryland. He also writes and tells city stories, many based on his
youth growing up in his family's beer garden–Adolph's Cafe–in the
Browntown section of Wilmington, Delaware.

Ed presents storytelling courses and writing workshops
based on his book *How to Conduct an Interview and Write an Original
Story*. With his wife, Kathleen, they present a popular workshop
entitled, "Self Publishing: All You Need to Know about Getting—or
Not Getting—into the Business."

About the Artist

K athleen Burgoon Okonowicz, a watercolor artist and illustrator, is originally from Greenbelt, Maryland. She studied
art in high school and college, and began focusing on real-
ism and detail more recently under Geraldine McKeown. She
enjoys taking things of the past and preserving them in her paintings.

Her first full-color, limited-edition print, *Special Places*,
features the stately stairway that was the "special place" of the
characters in Ed's love story, *Stairway over the Brandywine*.

A graduate of Salisbury State University, Kathleen earned
her master's degree in professional writing from Towson State
University. She is currently Publications Marketing Manager at the
International Reading Association in Newark, Delaware, and a
member of the Baltimore Watercolor Society.

**For information on other titles by Ed Okonowicz,
see pages 98 - 106.**

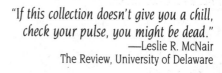

"If this collection doesn't give you a chill,
check your pulse, you might be dead."
—Leslie R. McNair
The Review, University of Delaware

"This expert storyteller can even make a
vanishing hitchhiker story fresh and startling.
Highly Recommended!"
—Chris Woodyard
Invisible Ink: Books on Ghosts & Hauntings

" 'Scary' Ed Okonowicz . . . the master of
written fear— at least on the Delmarva
Peninsula . . . has done it again."
—Wilmington News Journal

Storytelling World
Honor Award

"[Welcome Inn is] . . . a sort of auto-club guide
to ghosts, spirits and the unexplainable."
—Theresa Humphrey
Associated Press

Delaware Press Association
First Place Award

See order form on page 106.

$\mathcal{S}$pirits $\mathcal{B}$etween the $\mathcal{B}$ays Series

TRUE Ghost Stories

FROM THE
MASTER STORYTELLER

Ed Okonowicz

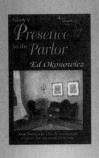

Delaware Press Association
First Place Award

This chilling series, invites you into a haunted house built upon ghostly tales of the Mid-Atlantic region.

Wander through the rooms, hallways, and dark corners of this eerie series.

Creep deeper and deeper into terror, until you run *Down the Stairs and Out the Door* in the last volume of our 13-book *Spirits* series.

**Volume by volume our
haunted house grows.
Enter at your own risk!**

Coming
next:
Vol. VIII
"Horror
in the
Hallway"

The Original

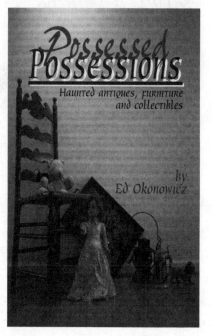

Possessed Possessions

Haunted antiques, furniture and collectibles

by Ed Okonowicz

A bump. A thud. Mysterious movement. Unexplained happenings. Caused by what? Venture beyond the Delmarva Peninsula and discover the answer. Experience 20 eerie, true tales, plus one horrifying fictional story, about items from across the country that, apparently, have taken on an independent *spirit* of their own–for they refuse to give up the ghost.

From Maine to Florida, from Pennsylvania to Wisconsin . . . haunted heirlooms exist among us . . . everywhere.

Read about them in **Possessed Possessions**, *the book some antique dealers definitely do not want you to buy.*

$9.95

112 pages
5 1/2 x 8 1/2 inches
softcover
ISBN 0-9643244-5-8

Now the sequel

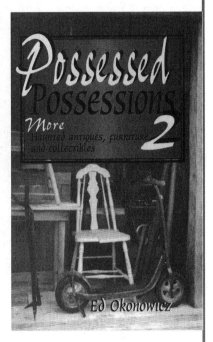

T hroughout the entire country, 'Possessed Possessions' continue to appear. Read about 40 more amazing true tales of bizarre, unusual and unexplained incidents—all caused by haunted objects including

Demented Dolls
Spirited Sculptures
Pesky Piano
Killer Crib—
and much, much more.

112 pages
5 1/2 x 8 1/2 inches
 softcover
ISBN 0-890690-02-3

$9.95

A
DelMarVa
Murder
Mystery

" . . . this is Okonowicz's
best book so far. "
—*The Star Democrat,*
Easton, Maryland

" [FIRED!] . . . produces
an interesting glimpse
into the high powered
world of politics with
kidnapping and murder
added for spice. "
—*Cecil Whig,*
Elkton, Maryland

"DelMarVa—
a dream state.
Pleasant for some; a
nightmare for others!"
—Tish Murzyn,
Atlantic Books,
Dover, Delaware

" . . . an entertaining, if gory, murder mystery. "
—*The Aegis,*
Harford County, Maryland

" . . . full of action, mystery, intrigue and
excitement. To call it a page turner
would be an understatement. "
—Linda Cutler Smith,
Mystery Group Coordinator,
Borders Books,
Wilmington, Delaware

Delaware Press Association
First Place Award

Get FIRED!

*I*t's early in the 21st century and DelMarVa, the newest state in the union is making headlines. There is full employment. Its residents pay no taxes. The crime rate is falling. And, with five casino-entertainment centers and a major theme park under construction, it's soon to be one of the country's top tourist destinations.

Just about everything is going right.

But, in the first year of this bold experiment in regional government, a serial kidnapper strikes . . . and the victims are a steadily growing number of DelMarVa residents.

Will the person the newspapers have dubbed "The Snatcher" ruin DelMarVa's utopian state? Or will the kidnapper be caught and swing from a noose at the end of a very stiff rope—since both hanging and the whipping post have been reinstated to eliminate crime on the peninsula.

In this first DelMarVa Murder Mystery, meet Governor Henry McDevitt, Police Commissioner Michael Pentak and state psychologist Dr. Stephanie Litera, as they pursue the peninsula's most horrifying kidnapper since the days of Patty Cannon.

320 pages
4 1/4 x 6 3/4 inches
softcover
ISBN 1-890690-01-5

$9.95

The DelMarVa Murder Mystery series continues as Governor Henry McDevitt and his colleagues solve another mystery in **Halloween House**. Coming in the Spring of 1999.

"For most of us, Disappearing Delmarva *is as close as we'll ever get to rubbing elbows with real treasure."*

—Brandywine Valley Weekly

Disappearing Delmarva introduces you to more than 70 people on the peninsula whose professions are endangered. Their work, words and wisdom are captured in the 208 pages of this hardbound volume, which features more than 60 photographs.

Along the back roads and back creeks of Delaware, Maryland and Virginia—in such hamlets as Felton and Blackbird in Delaware, Taylors Island and North East in Maryland, and Chincoteague and Sanford in Virginia—these colorful residents still work at the trades that have been passed down to them by grandparents and elders.

These people never made the news; they made America.

208 pp
8 1/2" x 11"
Hardcover
ISBN 1-890690-00-7

$38.00

Disappearing Delmarva

Portraits of the Peninsula People

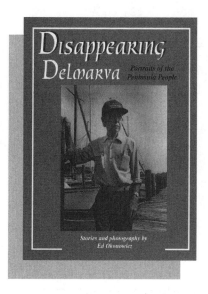

Photography and Stories by Ed Okonowicz

THE BUTLER, THE BAKER, THE FISHNET MAKER . . . ONCE FLOURISHING OCCUPATIONS ON THE DELMARVA PENINSULA . . . ARE A SAMPLING OF THE MANY SKILLS FALLING VICTIM TO TIME.

Winner of 2 First-Place Awards:

Best general book
Best photojournalism entry
National Federation of Press Women, Inc. 1998

Complete your collection...

or to be a part of the next book, complete the form below:

Name _____

Address _____

City _____ State _____ Zip Code _____

Phone Numbers (___) _____ (___) _____
                          Day   Evening

_____I would like to be placed on the mailing list to receive the free
Spirits Speaks newsletter and information on future volumes.

_____I have an experience I would like to share. Please call me.
(Each person who sends in a submission will be contacted. If your
story is used, you will receive a free copy of the volume in which
your experience appears.)

I would like to order the following books

Quantity	Title	Price	Total
	Pulling Back the Curtain, Vol. I	$8.95	
	Opening the Door, Vol. II	$8.95	
	Welcome Inn, Vol. III	$8.95	
	In the Vestibule, Vol. IV	$9.95	
	Presence in the Parlor, Vol. V	$9.95	
	Crying in the Kitchen, Vol. VI	$9.95	
	Up the Back Stairway, Vol. VII	**$9.95**	
	Possessed Possessions	$9.95	
	Possessed Possessions 2	$9.95	
	FIRED! A DelMarVa Murder Mystery	$9.95	
	Disappearing Delmarva	$38.00	
	Stairway over the Brandywine	$5.00	

*MD residents add 5% sales tax.   Subtotal _____
  Please include $1.50 postage for first book, Tax* _____
  and 50 cents for each additional book. Shipping _____
  Make checks payable to: Total _____
  Myst and Lace Publishers

All books are signed by the author. If you would like the book(s)
personalized, please specify to whom.

Mail to: Ed Okonowicz
             1386 Fair Hill Lane
             Elkton, MD 21921